The

Wee Musketeers

Robert Bresloff

The
Wee Musketeers

Robert Bresloff
Illustrated by Daniel Ziembo

An imprint of Gauthier Publications

1st Edition
<u>Proudly printed and bound in the USA</u>

Printed by McNaughton & Gunn
Saline, MI USA (January 2010)
Hungry Goat Press is an Imprint of Gauthier Publications
www.EataBook.com
Cover image by Daniel Ziembo
Cover design and layout by Elizabeth Gauthier
ISBN 13: 978-0-9820812-5-9

Library of Congress Cataloging-in-Publication Data

Bresloff, Robert.
 The wee musketeers / by Robert Bresloff ; illustrated by Daniel Ziembo.
   p. cm.
 Summary: Three eleven-year-old boys follow Grandpa Max into a magical
copy of The Three Musketeers to help him fix the story he has accidentally changed
 ISBN 978-0-9820812-5-9 (hardcover : alk. paper)
 [1. Magic--Fiction. 2. Grandfathers--Fiction. 3. Dumas, Alexandre, 1802-1870.
Three musketeers--Fiction.] I. Ziembo, Daniel, ill. II. Title.
 PZ7.B75455We 2010
 [Fic]--dc22   2009040716

To my Wee Musketeers, Nate and Audrey

Chapter One
The Three Musketeers

"**O**n guard!" cried Bobby, as he waved the crude wooden blade over his plumed hat. Bobby pushed at the wire rimmed glasses that had slid down his sweaty nose. He declared loudly, "No cardinal's guard is a good enough swordsman to match the great Athos!"

"Or Aramis!" chimed Keith. His dark eyes glowed with pride as they peered through the ragged plume that hung lazily from his hat.

Suddenly, a small, stocky figure burst out from behind a scraggy, nearly leafless bush and took his place between the others. It was Fritzy.

"I am Porthos," he cried in a raspy, game worn voice. "And we are—three!"

The three boys pretended to thrust and parry across the grassy field. Homemade uniforms flapped noisily in the breeze and wooden swords whistled as they cut through the wind. One by one the pretend foes fell or fled the brave trio's trusty swords. Athos was right— Athos was always right. The cardinal's guards were never any match for The Three Musketeers!

Onward throughout the day, the adventures of the three boys continued. Too busy to stop for lunch or even a soda, the battles raged on. Sometimes they lasted only minutes, at other times hours. It was 1961, and on summer days in Sky Harbor, one hour melted into the next. Time stood still, but the battles raged on.

The sun had fallen low in the sky and the boys' shadows had grown tall, far taller than their smaller, eleven year old bodies. Fritzy pulled off his musketeer's hat. He sneezed as part of the inexpensive, white, feathery plume crawled up his nose. The hat fell gently to the ground.

"What's wrong?" asked Bobby as he turned away from the fight. "Don't you want to play anymore?"

Fritzy rubbed some white fuzz from his nose with a quick swipe from the back of his hand.

"Aw… c'mon, Bobby," he sighed. "What are the Three Musketeers without D'Artagnan?"

Bobby tucked his wooden blade into a thick, black belt that his father thought he had thrown away.

"You know there's only you, me and Keith," replied Bobby impatiently. "We're the only kids for miles around."

Fritzy plopped onto the soft field grass, leaned back on his arms, and frowned. A soft breeze made his short blond hair bristle.

"I know!" he exclaimed. "But…well, it just isn't right without another kid to play D'Artagnan."

"Fritzy's right!" cried Keith as he also tossed his plumed hat onto the ground beside Fritzy's. He ran his hand through the dark curls that sat atop his narrow, pale face. "We need a D'Artagnan."

"My dad thinks that we're wasting the whole summer," continued Keith sorely. "He said that playing *The Three Musketeers* was dumb. He also said that your grandfather was a crazy old man!"

"Your dad thinks everything you do is dumb!" replied Bobby bitterly. "And my grandfather is not crazy!" He paused before pointing an accusing finger at Keith. "When he read the book to us you didn't think my grandfather was crazy!"

"Well…no…"

"You didn't think he was crazy when he taught us how to swordfight!"

"No…"

"You even thought it was pretty cool when he helped us make these musketeer uniforms—"

"Shut up," snapped Fritzy without even looking at his friends.

"Who're you tellin' to shut up?" growled Bobby. Fritzy and Keith jumped to their feet.

"Look Bobby," began Fritzy, in an oddly serious tone. Fritzy was the jokester of the three friends and his tone was rarely stern. Short and stocky, he sported a round freckled face with narrow slits that nearly hid his bright, blue eyes. "You have to admit that you're grandfather is… a little different."

"Yeah, that's what my dad said," snapped Keith.

Bobby shoved Keith's shoulder, forcing him back a step. "Your dad doesn't like anyone—"

"Bobby!" Fritzy shouted. "It's no more fun to pretend without D'Artagnan."

"Fritzy's right, Bobby," Keith added, "We need D'Artagnan."

Angry with his friends, Bobby pulled his three-cornered, plumed hat down over his ears, and hurried away.

"Hey," called Keith. "Where ya' goin'?"

Bobby didn't stop. He drew farther away from his friends.

"I'm going to ask my grandfather what we should do," he barked without looking back.

Keith and Fritzy gave each other a quick glance and started after Bobby.

"Wait up!" cried Fritzy. "We're coming, too!"

The path through the field to Bobby's house was well worn. Most times, the three friends could be found at Bobby's house since it was about halfway between Fritzy's and Keith's. The boys were always welcome. Bobby's mom was happy to make them all a tasty sandwich and a tall, cool drink on a hot summer's day.

There was another reason that the boys spent a lot of time at Bobby's—Bobby's grandfather. Grandpa Max lived in a cozy, little apartment that was built over the family's garage. Bobby's grandfather was well-read and a master storyteller. He wasn't very social. Grandpa Max rarely went out. Instead he preferred to spend his time with his books and reading to the boys. He would read to the kids for hours at a time.

"Do you really think your grandfather can help us find a D'Artagnan?" inquired Fritzy as Bobby's house came into view. "I mean…what could he possibly do?"

Bobby, not looking up from the path, shook his head. "I'm not sure," he replied softly. "But if anyone can help us, it's Grandpa Max!"

"Hey!" Keith grabbed both his friends by the arm. "I've got an idea."

Bobby and Fritzy turned reluctantly toward their friend. Keith was known to come up with some really hare-brained ideas. The two friends were prepared for the worst.

"Maybe," Keith continued thoughtfully, "your grandfather could introduce us to another book with only *three* main characters."

"Like what?' asked Fritzy.

"He's always talking about Sherlock Holmes," Keith quickly replied.

"There's only two main characters in those books, Sherlock Holmes and Dr. Watson," snapped Bobby.

"Oh, yeah," said Keith softly. "I forgot."

"Can we go now?" asked Fritzy.

Keith gave a thoughtful shrug before following his companions. Bobby's house was coming into view just beyond a familiar group of trees. The three boys had spent their entire lives in Sky Harbor and knew every inch of the small—even though *they* didn't find it so—charming town. A Piggly Wiggly, two gas stations, one diner, a drugstore and a tiny airport weren't enough to keep three boys with a lot of energy and imagination busy for very long.

The garage door was open but there was no sign of Bobby's mom or dad. Grandpa Max's narrow, wrinkled face filled the small window that overlooked the driveway from his small upstairs apartment.

Grandpa Max threw the window open and smiled. "C'mon up, boys," he said brightly. "I've been expecting you!"

Fritzy tapped Bobby's shoulder. "He's been expecting us?" he whispered with a shudder.

"How could he know we were coming?" inquired Keith softly. "We just—"

"Take it easy, guys," said Bobby. "I'm sure he's just kidding."

Bobby led the way up the wide wooden steps that led to Grandpa Max's apartment. The door swung open as they reached the top.

"Come in!" said Grandpa Max excitedly. "We need to talk about the problem."

Confused, the boys glanced quickly around from one to the other. Fritzy couldn't hold back.

"How could he know—?"

"Shhhhh!" hissed Bobby, quickly cutting him off.

"Come in, come in!" cried Grandpa Max. "We need to talk about D'Artagnan!"

"Uh, Bobby…how did he know…?" said Keith, his voice quickly trailing off.

"Shhhhh!" Bobby hissed again.

The boys got stuck, shoulder to shoulder, as they

all tried to squeeze through the doorway at the same time. Grandpa Max threw up his hands and grabbed two of the boy's arms, not really caring whose arms they were, and dragged them all into the room.

"Come in, come in!" cried Bobby's grandfather. "There isn't much time!"

"How did you know we were coming to see you?" asked Bobby.

"Oh that," replied Grandpa Max. "That was easy. You boys always come by the house about this time for a snack."

The boys gave a collective sigh of relief. Grandpa Max seemed to be more aware of their habits than they were. But something wasn't quite right. Bobby's grandfather seemed agitated and nervous. He appeared to be wearing a costume similar to theirs. Bobby couldn't remember his grandfather ever acting this way before. His face contorted with dread, the old man paced back and forth across the floor of his tidy apartment.

"What is it, Grandpa?" inquired Bobby as Grandpa Max paced toward him. He looked into his grandfather's bright blue, still youthful eyes. Grandpa Max shot the boy a brief smile before a frown painted over his face.

"It's D'Artagnan, Bobby," he began nervously. "He's in trouble."

"He's always in trouble," said Fritzy with a snort. "If he wasn't, the book would be really boring—"

Grandpa Max dismissed Fritzy with a curt wave of his hand. "No, no!" he exclaimed. "He's *really* in trouble!"

Bobby grasped his grandfather's bony elbow and said,

"Maybe you should sit down Grandpa."

Grandpa Max pulled his arm from the boy's gentle grasp. "Don't you understand?" he snapped. "It's my fault!"

"What's your fault?" asked Bobby.

Grandpa Max sank into his dark leather chair, dug his elbows into his knees and buried his face deeply into knuckled hands.

"Athos, Porthos and Aramis are being held by the cardinal's guards so they cannot help D'Artagnan reach London and the Duke of Buckingham."

Keith looked at Bobby and Fritzy while he twirled his finger alongside his ear and mouthed 'cuckoo'. Bobby narrowed his eyes and Keith stopped.

"But, Grandpa, that's not how the book goes—"

Bobby was quickly cut off.

"I know!" snapped the old man. "And it's entirely my fault."

Grandpa Max sprang from his chair and paced across the room.

"I've got to go back," he continued thoughtfully. "I must go back and set things right."

"Go where?" asked Bobby.

"Back to Paris! Back to 1626!" he replied. "Back into the book!"

"What book, Grandpa?"

"*The Three Musketeers*, Bobby, haven't you been listening?"

CHAPTER TWO
Grandpa Max

The boys whispered nervously to each other as they crept down the stairs. Unnerved by Grandpa Max's odd behavior, they slipped out of the apartment while Bobby's grandfather went off on another tangent about D'Artagnan. The old man did not even notice that they had left.

"You know what, Bobby?" whispered Fritzy. Bobby looked at Fritzy and raised his eyebrows. "I think your grandpa really might be crazy!"

Bobby didn't reply.

"Fritzy's right," added Keith. "What in the world did he mean about going to Paris in 1626?"

Bobby stopped at the bottom of the stairs and heaved a great sigh. "Yeah," he finally said. "I think maybe I should tell my mom about how he's acting." Bobby shuddered. "That was out there, even for Grandpa Max."

"I think he's cuckoo," said Keith. Again, he twirled a finger at his head.

"Shut up, Keith!" exclaimed Bobby, while rubbing a tear from his reddening eyes. "He's just old. Sometimes old people get a little funny, that's all."

Bobby urged his friends to wait outside while he went in to tell his mother about Grandpa Max's strange behavior. He'd only been in the house for a short time before his mother stormed out the back door and headed for the stairs that led up to Grandpa Max's apartment. Bobby followed her out of the house and joined his friends on the driveway.

"Boy," commented Keith as Bobby's mother, wearing a pink housecoat and hair curlers, hurried up the stairs. "That was fast."

"Mom's been worried about Grandpa Max for a while," said Bobby as his mother disappeared into the garage apartment.

"How long has he been acting funny?" inquired Fritzy.

"About a month," replied Bobby. "Dad noticed that he'd been dressing in funny costumes—"

"Hey!" Fritzy grabbed Bobby's arm. "Now that you mentioned it, what was your grandpa wearing? It looked kinda' like our musketeer outfits—"

"BOBBY!" Fritzy was quickly interrupted by Bobby's mother's shrill call. "Where's your grandfather?" she asked stepping out the door onto the staircase.

Bobby's nose wrinkled. "What?" he cried. "He's up in the apartment, Mom."

"I'm not in the mood for games, young man—"

"Honest, Mom," Bobby pleaded, "we just left him."

"Really, Mrs. B," added Fritzy. "Me and Keith have been out here the whole time—"

Bobby's mom rushed down the stairs.

"I'm calling the police!" she snapped, as she reached the bottom step. "Your grandfather is missing!"

"Wow," breathed Keith, "the cops!"

"*Who's* missing?" cracked a voice from the landing at the top of the stairs.

Bobby swung around. "Grandpa!" he exclaimed brightly.

Bobby's mother looked up at her father in disbelief. "Dad?" she gasped. "But…I…where *were* you?"

Grandpa Max smiled and shrugged.

"I was in the closet organizing my books—"

"Why didn't you answer when I called?"

Grandpa rubbed his square chin thoughtfully before gently tapping at his ear.

"Sorry," Max chuckled. "I wasn't wearing my hearing aid. You know I can't hear a thing without it."

"But, Grandpa," said Bobby, "You had—"

"Yes, Bobby," Grandpa Max quickly interrupted his grandson, "I am wearing it now—just put it in." The old man's eyes twinkled.

"Bobby!" Fritzy hissed through clenched teeth.

"I know," he replied from the corner of his mouth. "He heard *us* just fine."

Bobby's mother stood at the bottom of the stairway

glaring up at her father. "You scared me half to death," she scolded. "Please remember to wear your hearing aid."

"I promise," he said brightly. "Good day, dear. See you tomorrow boys." The door shut tightly behind him.

*   *   *

Bobby stared out his window. Ribbons of orange streaked the grayish-blue sky signaling another day quickly coming to a close. He sighed as he glanced across the driveway toward his grandfather's dark apartment. Bobby's mind wandered to Grandpa Max's peculiar behavior.

Sure, his grandfather was bit strange. He lived for reading his books. Only the classics for Grandpa Max—Jules Verne, Alexandre Dumas, Sir Arthur Conan Doyle, H.G. Wells—he didn't like modern authors. He literally buried himself in those old books.

Bobby had barely looked away from his grandpa's shadowy window when a light in the apartment blinked on. He eyed Grandpa Max's silhouette against the window shade. Bobby jumped from his bed and ran down the stairs. In a flash, he appeared at the apartment's doorway. The door opened slowly before Bobby even knocked.

"Grandpa?" he whispered as he peered into what looked to be an empty apartment. There was no answer. Bobby took one cautiously placed step over the threshold.

"Bobby!" Grandpa Max cried brightly as he popped out from behind the open door. Bobby was so startled he nearly leaped out of his pajamas. He grabbed his chest, gasping for air.

"Grandpa," he said breathlessly. "You scared me!"

"Oh…sorry," replied his grandfather. Bobby looked up; the old man still had that twinkle in his eye. "Come in, come in." Grandpa Max grabbed the boy's arm and led him into the room. Bobby heard the door snap shut behind him.

"What's going on, Grandpa?" asked Bobby.

Grandpa Max ignored Bobby and rushed toward the window. "Shhhhh!" he hissed loudly as he peeked around the closed curtains. "Where's your mother?"

"C'mon Grandpa, what was all that stuff about D'Artagnan and Paris? And why did you lie to Mom about your hearing aid? Are you in some kind of trouble?"

Grandpa Max turned away from the window.

"What time is it?" he asked excitedly.

Bobby shrugged. "I don't know," he replied. "Nine, nine-thirty? Why?"

Bobby's grandfather snatched a book from the top of the nightstand next to his bed and started for the closet.

"Can't talk," snapped his grandfather. "Must go—"

"Go where?"

"Didn't I tell you," he said impatiently. "I must help D'Artagnan!"

Bobby grabbed Grandpa Max's arm.

"Please tell me what this is all about, Grandpa Max?" he pleaded. "Pleeease!"

Grandpa Max heaved a great sigh.

"Only if you promise not to tell *anyone*," he replied, "*especially* your mother."

Bobby nodded enthusiastically. "What about Fritzy and Keith?"

Grandpa Max rubbed his chin thoughtfully. "Only if they take the Musketeer's oath," replied the old man with a wink.

Bobby nodded again.

"Excellent!" exclaimed Grandpa Max. "Now, sit down and I'll explain everything."

CHAPTER THREE
All for One—One For All

"That's impossible!" cried Bobby.

"No it's not," retorted Grandpa Max. Then leaning in, very close to Bobby, he whispered, "I've done it. I mean... I do it."

Bobby drew in a deep breath, unsure of what to say. Imagine his surprise. Bobby's grandfather had just told him that he could travel into books and actually interact with the characters. Bobby loved Grandpa Max dearly. But even *he* had to admit that his grandfather had been acting strange lately. A bit eccentric, maybe a little scatterbrained, but this was more than he could stand.

"Okay, Grandpa," he began, trying very hard to control the impatience in his voice. "How?"

Grandpa Max sat up and walked toward the small closet where he kept all his wonderful books stacked neatly on homemade shelves.

"The secret's in there, Bobby," he said softly. "In the closet."

Bobby jumped up and shuffled across the room. His slippers made a swooshing sound against the thickly piled carpet. He peeked into the small, familiar storage room that he had been in so many times before. He sniffed the all too familiar smell of old books and magazines.

"But how, Grandpa," he asked suspiciously. "I've been in this closet a thousand times—"

"I know, Bobby, I know. But something very mysterious happened about two months ago—"

"What happened?"

"I'm not exactly sure—"

"Grandpa!"

Grandpa Max stepped into the closet and pulled the chain attached to the single, naked bulb fixture on the ceiling.

"You see," he began while removing a thin volume from the top shelf. "One night, I went to take this book from the shelf—"

"What book is that?" inquired Bobby.

"*The Hound of the Baskervilles,*" he replied.

"Sherlock Holmes? Me and the guys liked that one almost as much as *The Three Musketeers.*"

"I know," said Grandpa Max brightly. "It's the best known Sherlock Holmes mystery."

"Grandpa," said Bobby softly, trying to get his attention.

"A fascinating adventure…" Grandpa Max continued as if Bobby hadn't said a word.

Bobby spoke a little louder. "Grandpa!"

"… The novel that made Sherlock Holmes one of the most famous names in lit—"

"GRANDPA!" shouted Bobby.

Grandpa Max shook his head. "Oh dear," he said softly, "I do get carried away."

Bobby pointed at the book.

"Yes," continued Grandpa Max, "the book, of course. You see, I grabbed the wrong book, realized my mistake and went to replace it. Then, when I took down *The Hound of the Baskervilles…*"

"What?" Bobby asked eagerly.

"When I took down *The Hound of Baskervilles* I dropped the book on the floor. Clumsy of me, I really wasn't paying att—"

"Then what?"

"Oh yes, yes, The book fell to the floor and opened to this page."

Grandpa Max's bony fingers fumbled with the tiny volume for a moment before finally coming to the page he was looking for.

"Yes, yes," he said thoughtfully, "here's the page…read the very top."

Bobby tugged at the book but Grandpa Max wouldn't let go.

"You can read it out loud, Bobby," his grandfather cautioned, "but do not touch the book when you do."

Bobby reluctantly released his grip on the book and cocked his head so he could see the page better. "Let's see," he said softly, "it says, 'Chapter Two, The Curse of the Baskervilles.'" Bobby looked up into his grandfather's bright, blue eyes. "So?"

"So," replied Grandpa Max, "I picked up the book, and as I did, I read those same words and whoosh, the closet suddenly disappeared. I found myself in the sitting room of none other than *the* Mr. Sherlock Holmes of 221B Baker Street in London, England.. Bobby shot his grandfather an incredulous look before stepping backward out of the closet.

"You don't believe me, do you Bobby?"

"Uh…I." Bobby didn't know what to say,

"Remember," said his grandfather sternly, "you promised me that you wouldn't tell your mother."

"I know, but…"

"You promised."

"Okay. But, Grandpa, this sounds crazy—"

"How in the world do you think I know so much about the characters from the books that I read to you and your friends?"

"I…uh…"

"Where do you think I go when you come looking for me and I'm not here?"

"Uh… the park feeding the pigeons?"

"I hate pigeons—dirty, dirty birds. No, Bobby, I travel into the books. It's wonderful…" Grandpa Max grabbed Bobby's wrist looking for a watch that wasn't there. "What time is it?" he inquired hastily.

"About ten I guess," replied Bobby. "But what's the difference—?"

"Go home, Bobby!" exclaimed Grandpa Max. "Go home and go to bed. We'll talk about this tomorrow."

Bobby scratched at his head through his sun-bleached hair and turned toward the door.

"And remember," continued his grandfather, "not a word of this to your mother."

Bobby walked down the stairs slowly. Tears filled his young eyes. Grandpa Max was as much a friend as a loved one. Bobby swore that he wouldn't tell his mom about his grandfather, but he wasn't sure that a secret like this should be kept from her. But he *did* promise.

No problem, he thought as he watched the light in Grandpa Max's apartment fade, *I'm sure Grandpa Max will be his old self in the morning.*

"Yeah," he said to himself softly. "I'm sure he will."

The next day was the same as yesterday in Sky Harbor. To the three eleven year old boys, the small Midwestern town's days seemed to last forever. There wasn't much to do on these long summer days and Grandpa Max's problem had melted into the landscape of green fields and trees. After the boys tired of watching the single engine Cessna airplanes take off, they started to play musketeers. But the battles lacked the vigor they once had. After an hour or so, with their enthusiasm gone, the boys became bored with the game.

"I'm going home!" exclaimed Keith bitterly. "This isn't fun anymore."

"Oh come on, you big baby," teased Bobby, "one more duel—"

"He's right, Bobby," snapped Fritzy, cutting Bobby off cold. "I'm bored."

"Aw, c'mon, guys," Bobby pleaded. "Just one more game. It's almost dinner time."

Fritzy gathered up his hat and his trusty wooden sword. "Hey Bobby," he began, "how's Grandpa Max doing?"

Bobby blushed brightly behind his wire rim glasses. Even his ears felt warm.

"Is he okay?" inquired Keith.

Bobby hesitated a moment, unsure of what to say.

"Okay," snapped Fritzy. "Don't tell us—"

"Okay! Okay," said Bobby raising his voice. "I'll tell you, but you have to take the Musketeer's oath *and* promise not to tell anyone."

Fritzy and Keith shot each other a glance.

"Sure, no problem," said Fritzy.

"No problem," echoed Keith.

Bobby held out his right hand and smiled. Keith and Fritzy placed their hands on top of his.

"All for one!" cried Bobby.

"One for all!" they sang out in unison.

Bobby told them everything his grandfather had told him the night before. Except for an occasional gasp from Keith or burp from Fritzy, Bobby's friends didn't say a word until their friend had finished. Bobby sighed; the Musketeer's oath of secrecy had been sealed. He knew he could depend on Fritzy and Keith. Grandpa Max's secret would be safe forever.

The boys had just started up the stone driveway when Bobby's mother burst from the house. Bobby turned pale and stopped dead in his tracks.

"Uh-oh, Bobby" said Keith without moving his lips, "looks like you're in trouble."

"Yeah, man," added Fritzy .

"I think I hear my mother calling," said Keith cupping his hand behind his ear.

"Me too," giggled Fritzy.

"C'mon, guys," whispered Bobby as his mother stormed nearer. "Don't go. She won't yell at me if you guys are here."

"BOBBY!" shouted his mother.

"You're dead," observed Fritzy. "It's been nice knowing you—"

"Have you seen Grandpa Max?" she cried.

Bobby let out a big sigh of relief. The color flushed quickly back to his cheeks.

"Uh…no Mom," he stammered. "What's wrong?"

"Your grandfather's missing again."

"Maybe he went for a walk, Mrs. B," suggested Keith.

"No," she replied while running her fingers through short, blond hair. It was obvious Bobby's mother was upset. Her deeply tanned face appeared ashen and cold. "I saw him go up to his apartment—I had forgotten to give him a message so I followed him up…"

"Then what, Mom?" asked Bobby.

"He wasn't there—again."

"Aww, he probably just slipped out when you weren't looking, Mrs. B," Fritzy assured her. "You want us to look around the neighborhood?"

"No," she said thoughtfully, "I'll do that. I can cover more ground in the car. You boys wait in the apartment. If he comes home, I'm counting on you three to keep him here until I get back."

As Bobby's mother backed the car down the driveway, the boys quickly made their way up the steps and into Grandpa Max's apartment. The small set of rooms seemed gloomy without Bobby's grandfather's cheery presence. Bobby opened the closet door.

"Gee, Bobby," said Keith, "I never really noticed all the stuff your grandfather had until now."

Fritzy ran his hand gently along a shelf that ran across the closet's long wall, just across from the door.

"Yeah," he commented. "Look at all this junk."

Bobby had to admit that he had never really given the shelf more than a quick glance. His grandfather was very secretive about the closet. The boys lined up in front of the dusty shelf.

"You know," Bobby began thoughtfully, "Grandpa Max never talked much about the closet, except for the books."

"Hey!" exclaimed Fritzy, snatching a dusty black smoking pipe from the shelf. "I didn't know Grandpa Max smoked a pipe."

"He doesn't… at least I don't think he does…" said Bobby. "Can I see that?"

Bobby stared at the pipe's dark, grainy surface. There was a curious paper tag attached to the long stem.

"Hey!" cried Keith. "Look at this big seashell!"

Bobby glanced up, but it was too late to stop him. Keith

Robert Bresloff

had snatched the shiny, tan shell from the shelf.

"Now why would your grandfather…" Keith's voice faded.

"What's wrong?" asked Fritzy.

"There's an inscription—"

"Let me see that!" snapped Bobby before carefully grasping the shell with his free hand.

"*To Max*," he said softly reading the brass plaque that had been affixed to the shell. "*Thank you for all your help. The crew of the Nautilus and I will be forever in your debt. Signed, Captain Nemo.*"

"Captain Nemo, from *Twenty Thousand Leagues Under the Sea*?" asked Keith incredulously.

"Bobby, look," gasped Fritzy. "There's something written on the tag that's hanging off the pipe!"

Bobby handed the shell back to Keith. Pulling the pipe closer, he read what was written on the tag out loud, "*Thank you for your invaluable assistance during Doctor Watson's unexpected absence. Signed, S. Holmes.*"

"Sherlock Holmes?" gasped Keith.

"I think your Grandpa Max might *be* crazy Bobby," said Fritzy in a hushed tone.

"No he's not!" cried Bobby.

"Then, why would he make up stuff like this?"

Bobby stepped out of the closet and sat on the bed. Fritzy followed.

"Do you really think that Grandpa Max is crazy?" Bobby asked in a soft and troubled voice.

"I don't know, Bobby," replied Fritzy. "But making

stuff like this up can't be too normal. People can't travel into books!"

"I guess you're right—"

"Bobby!" cried Keith who was still in the closet. Bobby and Fritzy turned as their friend burst through the doorway and dropped onto the bed. "Look! It's an envelope and it's addressed to you." Keith handed the tiny white envelope to Bobby.

Bobby removed a small scrap of folded paper and opened it. He shook his head upon reading his grandfather's scratchy writing.

"What does it say?" asked Fritzy.

Bobby handed the note to Keith, who read it out loud.

"*Bobby,*" he began nervously, "*If you are reading this note then you are probably in the closet. Remove 'The Three Musketeers' and open it to the page that I have marked. Grandpa Max.*"

Bobby shot up from the bed and went to the closet. "Here it is!" he exclaimed as he found his grandfather's ancient copy of *The Three Musketeers*. When Bobby opened the book another scrap of paper dropped to the floor. He quickly snatched it up.

"It says," said Bobby eagerly. "*Recite these words while the book is open to this page and join me in Paris, 1626. You'll meet the real D'Artagnan!*"

"Okay, Bobby," snapped Fritzy. "I think you'd better tell your mom all about this—"

"Let's try it," Bobby snapped back.

"Try what?" asked Keith.

"Going into the book."

"You're as crazy as your grandfather!" exclaimed Fritzy.

"What's the matter Fritzy, you chicken?" teased Bobby.

"No way!" replied Fritzy. "It's impossible."

"How do you know?"

"You are crazy!"

"If it's impossible, what have you got to lose?"

Fritzy narrowed his eyes at Bobby.

"Okay, I'll do it."

Keith threw up his hands.

"You're both crazy!" he cried. "I'm getting out of here."

"What about *The Three Musketeers*, Keith?"

"That's just a story, Bobby."

Fritzy grabbed the note. "Is this what we have to say?" he asked.

"That's what it says," replied Bobby.

"C'mon, Keith," said Fritzy, "Let's give it a try."

Keith glanced at Fritzy then at Bobby. Both boys smiled widely at their friend.

"Okay," he replied softly. "But I have to be home by five."

Bobby and Fritzy started to laugh.

"Okay, by five," chuckled Bobby. "Is everybody ready?"

The two friends gave Bobby a reluctant nod.

"ALL FOR ONE!" exclaimed Bobby.

Then the three friends shouted loudly, "ONE FOR ALL!"

Chapter Four
The Bakery

The boys clutched each others hands tightly. The tiny closet began to spin. Around and around and around the boys spun, making the books and shelves blur from view.

"Whoaaaaaa!" cried Fritzy.

"What's happening?" shrieked Keith.

"I-I-I-don't know," replied Bobby, who was as frightened as his friends.

Faster and faster the closet spun. Everything turned to black and became as cold as a winter's night.

"Brrrrrr!" Fritzy cried with a shiver.

"Why is it so cold?" squeaked Keith.

"I-I-I don't know," repeated Bobby.

"Is that all you can say?" Fritzy asked impatiently.

"I-I-I don't know."

"HELP!" screamed Fritzy. His voice echoed into the cold blackness.

Their world spun faster yet.

"I think I'm going to hurl!" shrieked Keith.

"You better not!" shouted Fritzy.

"HELP!" shouted Keith.

When it seemed as if it could get neither darker nor colder, the spinning room came to an abrupt halt, sending the boys sprawling onto a warm wooden floor.

Keith gave the rough wooden planks beneath him a big kiss. "I'm glad that's over," he said breathlessly.

Fritzy sat up and looked around. "It sure doesn't smell like Grandpa Max's closet," he commented while rubbing his still frigid arms. "It's so dark. Who turned out the lights?"

"What *is* that smell, Bobby?" asked Keith. "Is your mom baking cookies?"

Bobby took two or three short whiffs of the air. "Even if she was, we wouldn't smell it up here," he said cautiously. "And besides, Mom's out looking for Grandpa Max—"

"Shush!" hissed Fritzy. "Do you hear singing?"

Bobby listened. Yes, there was singing. A deep baritone voice was echoing brightly through the dark.

"I think it's coming from outside the closet."

"Do you think it's Grandpa Max?" asked Fritzy.

"Do you think we're still in the closet?" inquired Keith. "It's so dark, I can't see a thing."

Bobby stood and peered around into the darkness. Before long, his eyes came to rest upon a slight crack of light at floor level— *a door*.

"There's only one way to find out," said Bobby, as he moved toward the faint crack of light.

Searching for a doorknob, Bobby clumsily fumbled above the crack of light. Within seconds, he could feel the cool brass against his skin. Small beads of sweat began forming on Bobby's forehead as he turned the knob gently to the right. A soft click filled his ears. The singing stopped.

"It's a door," whispered Bobby. "Come here quick."

"Come where?" asked Fritzy. "I can't see you."

"Look at the floor. Can you see the light?" Bobby continued to whisper.

"Yeah," Fritzy replied softly.

"I'm going to open the door and let some more light in—"

The singing started again. The beautiful voice sounded low and smooth. Bobby pulled the door open an inch. The soft song ceased again.

"Who is there?" asked the deep voice. "Who sneaks around my bakery?"

"Bakery!" whispered Fritzy.

"Shush!" hissed Bobby. He felt the goose bumps erupt up and down his arms.

"Ahhhh," purred the voice. "It would seem that I have yet another visitor. Come out. Come out. All are welcomed at *my* establishment."

Bobby took a deep breath and pressed his hand against the door. It swung open slowly. Fritzy and Keith wasted no time pushing him through the half opened doorway.

"So," said the voice. "I see that my visitor is a young

man… and dressed as a king's musketeer at that."

Bobby blinked against the brightly lit kitchen. Once his eyes adjusted to the light, his gaze quickly found the person who possessed the smooth, low voice. Large and round with an equally robust, pink face, the man was dressed in white from head to toe.

"Come in my little friend. Come in," said the man brightly. "You must be hungry after your long trip."

"Long trip?" Bobby questioned.

"Oui," replied the jovial figure. "You did not come in the front door and the only way in or out of that room is the doorway behind you. So, I assume you have traveled from a place far, far away." The man gave Bobby a smile and a wink.

"Look," began Bobby as he looked in amazement at the old fashioned hearths and ovens. "I don't know where I am or who you are. I'm just looking for my grandfather—"

"Ahhhh," said the man pleasantly. "You must mean Monsieur Max."

"You know my grandfather?"

"But of course…" The round man made a questioning gesture with his outstretched hands.

"Bobby," said Bobby when he realized that the man wanted to know his name.

"Ah then, Monsieur Bobby," said the man with a nod. "You will come and eat first, and then we will talk of your grandfather." He gestured once again but this time it was toward a table filled with puffy, powdery pastries. "Come, please enjoy one of my cream puffs."

"Cream puffs!" cried Keith from inside the still

darkened storeroom.

"Shush!" hissed Fritzy.

The man took one step toward the door and smiled.

"I see that you are not alone," said the smiling baker. "Come out, boys. There is more than enough for all of you."

Fritzy and Keith shuffled through the doorway into the warm kitchen.

"Wow!" cried Keith, his eyes as large and round as glazed donuts. "Look at those cream puffs!"

"Ah, there are three, wee musketeers." The man shot Bobby a sideways glance and smiled broadly. "There are only three, correct?"

Bobby nodded.

"Then come and enjoy, my little musketeers," he said as he briskly rubbed his pudgy hands together. "Eat as many of Xavier's pastries as you like."

Keith quickly tore into a very large, round, powdery cream puff while Bobby and Fritzy gazed in wonderment at the old fashioned kitchen. Brightly lit gas lanterns lined the rough stone walls. Ovens made of reddish brick filled each corner of the room. The smell of baked pastries belched from the fiery ovens, sending a heavy but sweet scent into the air.

Fritzy joined Keith at the table filled with wonderful sweets, but Bobby couldn't think of food. He desperately needed to know more about what had happened to Grandpa Max.

"You know my grandfather, Max?" inquired Bobby.

A wide smile split Xavier's pleasant, round face.

"But, of course," he replied brightly. "Max is a frequent

and welcomed visitor to this establishment."

"Bobby!" cried Keith as he stuffed another succulent puff eagerly into his mouth. "Youf ga ta twy sum ov deez."

Bobby snickered as he glanced at his powdery faced friends who were certainly enjoying the pastries. "Can you tell me where my grandfather is?" he said turning back to their new friend.

Xavier gave Bobby a nonchalant wave of his thick, flour covered hand.

"I am certain your grandfather is off gallivanting with that rascal, D'Artagnan!" exclaimed Xavier.

"D'Artagnan!" cried Bobby.

"Yes," said Xavier. "The young Gascon and Max get along famously—"

"What do you mean D'Artagnan?" inquired Fritzy after gulping down one last bite of cream puff. "D'Artagnan the musketeer?"

"No, no," responded Xavier, his head shaking quickly back and forth. "D'Artagnan is not yet a musketeer, but someday—"

"Phew," sighed Fritzy. "For a second there I thought we might really be in Paris."

Xavier laughed loudly. His thick rosy cheeks flushed brightly.

"What's so funny?" asked Bobby.

"But, my little musketeers, you *are* in Paris."

"Don't tell me it's 1626," snickered Keith.

"Oui," said Xavier, still grinning broadly.

"We, what?" inquired Bobby.

"Oui, it *is* 1626," replied Xavier.

"This is too weird, Bobby!" exclaimed Fritzy. "It can't be 1626—"

"1626!" cried Keith. "I've got to be home by five. My dad's going to kill me."

"Relax," said Bobby with a laugh, "if it's really 1626, you're way early—"

"That's not funny, Bobby—"

"Keith's right!" Fritzy grabbed Bobby by the arm. "If this is Paris in 1626, how're we going to get home?"

Xavier laughed out loud again.

"Why," he began, "the same way you came, of course."

"What?" cried Bobby. "We're not even sure how we got here!"

"It cannot be that difficult. Monsieur Max comes and goes all the time, my little friends."

"I'm going to find Grandpa Max," declared Bobby loudly.

"Good idea," agreed Fritzy.

"Yeah," said Keith. "Let's find your grandfather."

The three boys marched out of the kitchen.

"I would not do that, little ones," Xavier warned. "The Cardinal's Guards, they are everywhere these days,"

"Don't worry about us," replied Keith. "We can take care of ourselves."

"But the Cardinal's Guards…"

It was too late; the boys had left the kitchen and were headed for the bakery's front door.

"Wait, my little musketeers," shouted Xavier. "It's dark

and dangerous out there…"

The boys had already made it out to the gas-lit, cobblestone street. The night felt chilly. Keith and Fritzy rubbed their upper arms briskly.

"I don't know how your grandpa pulled this off Bobby, but this is really cool," said Fritzy.

"Cool?" exclaimed Keith. "Bobby, I'm scared."

"Aw, c'mon," snapped Fritzy. "You don't think this is real do you? Grandpa Max is playing a trick on us."

"I'm not so sure Fritzy," replied Bobby. "This all seems pretty real."

"Yeah right," said Fritzy as he looked up and down the narrow, shop-lined street. "I bet your mom's in on it, too."

"I'm scared," Keith said softly. There was a distinct shiver to his voice.

"Me too," commented Bobby. "I think we're really here."

"Where? Paris in 1626?" scoffed Fritzy.

"Yeah, we are!"

"I'm scared," Keith said louder.

"We heard you, Keith," snapped Fritzy. "Stop acting like a little baby—"

"Give him a break!" shouted Bobby. "I'm just as scared as he—"

"You there!" a gruff voice echoed loudly from down the street. The boy's heads snapped in that direction.

"What are you boys doing out this late?" boomed another voice. "Do not move!"

"Can you see anything, Bobby?" asked Fritzy trying to

see into the darkness.

"Not yet," he replied. "But it sounds like footsteps are heading our way."

"L-L-Let's go back in the bakery," said Keith, his voice trembling even more.

"Good idea," agreed Bobby. "I don't like the sound of this—"

"Aw, c'mon guys," razzed Fritzy. "The whole thing's a joke. Grandpa Max is going to step out of the dark and say 'boo' any second—"

"You there!" shouted a third voice. "Do not move!"

"Oh," laughed Fritzy loudly, "this is really good. Your grandfather's the best—"

Three large men dressed in the red and black caped uniforms of the Cardinal's Guard emerged from the darkness. All three wore fully brimmed, black hats topped with flowing, red plumes. Each sported cleanly trimmed mustaches that curled upward gracefully at the ends. Broad smiles split their pale faces just below these wisps of hair.

"Oh look," said the largest of the three. "They are dressed as little musketeers."

"Ha!" laughed another. "I suppose we should be afraid of these three."

Unfazed by what was occurring Fritzy boldly stepped forward. "The Cardinal's Guards are never a match for the King's Musketeers!" he exclaimed proudly.

Bobby snatched a handful of Fritzy's sleeve and yanked him around.

"What are you doing?" Bobby cried.

"Hey, cool it, Bobby," replied Fritzy. "I'm just playing along, that's all."

"Come along, boys," said the largest of the three men. "I think it's time to go home. Where do you live?"

"Uh…" Bobby didn't know what to say.

"Take us to Captain de Treville's," snapped Fritzy while trying to keep a straight face.

Captain de Treville was the captain of the King's Musketeers. D'Artagnan, Athos, Porthos and Aramis were his favorites of all the musketeers.

"Fritzy!" snarled Keith. "Cool it!"

"Won't tell us where you live, eh?" snapped one of the guards. This one had a large, red bulbous nose. "What should we do with these little musketeers?" he asked, turning to the biggest of the three.

"To the orphanage, I suppose," he replied. "Yes, the orphanage."

"Orphanage this!" cried Fritzy as he hauled off and kicked the smallest guard in the shin.

"Ouch!" cried the guard. "Why you—"

"Get them!" screamed the larger man.

Fritzy drew the wooden sword that was tucked into his tattered belt and waved it wildly at the three men.

"All for one!" he shouted.

Bobby and Keith drew their swords and joined their comrade.

"One for all!" they shouted back.

"What should we do?" asked the guard while attempting to rub the pain from his skinned shin.

"I said take them to the orphanage!" growled the big nosed leader.

"You'll never take us alive!" Fritzy called out brightly.

Bobby and Keith turned, each giving Fritzy a look of disbelief.

The three guards drew their swords. Bobby and Keith grabbed Fritzy and stepped backwards.

"What's the matter, guys?" he chided as his friends pulled him back.

"I think these guys are for real, Fritzy," said Bobby. "I think we'd better get back inside the bakery and find Xavier."

The guards matched the boy's backward movement.

"Bobby's right!" exclaimed Keith. "L-L-Let's get out of here."

"You will drop your swords and come with us, little musketeers!" growled the large guard. The man's eyes narrowed as he dropped the point of his sword onto Fritzy's chest. Fritzy felt the sharp tip nearly pierce his skin.

"Gulp!" swallowed Fritzy. "You know, guys," he whispered, "Maybe you're right. Let's get out of here—"

"HOLD!" cried another voice from the darkness. "Do the Cardinal's Guards engage in duels with children now? Let those boys go or you will pay dearly!"

The boys looked over their shoulders. Their eyes strained against the darkness to see who had come to save them.

"Who dares to threaten His Eminence's Guards?" snapped the large nosed guard.

A man stepped under the light of the gas lamp. He was

dressed all in blue and quickly removed his short cap. Then he drew his sword.

"We dare!" he cried, waving his sword. The shiny steel glittered softly against the dim street light. "My sword and I!"

CHAPTER FIVE
D'Artagnan

"It's D'Artagnan!" whispered Bobby, staring at the man's shadowy features.

"That's impossible," replied Fritzy. "D'Artagnan's just a character in a book."

"He looks just like the book described him."

"I don't care who he is as long as he can keep these goons from taking us away," said Keith.

"Good thought," agreed Bobby.

As the young swordsman stepped closer to the light, his handsome, narrow, mustached face became visible to the guards. The three men raised their swords, pointing them menacingly at the intruder. The large guard with the big nose spoke first.

"Be gone, brigand!" he cried. "Leave these street urchins to us."

"The boys are with me," replied the stranger. "I will

take full responsibility—"

"By whose authority?" cried the guard.

"His Majesty's Guard!" replied the handsome stranger.

Bobby tugged eagerly at Fritzy's sleeve. "I told you it was D'Artagnan," he snapped. "D'Artagnan was in the King's Guard before the Cardinal commissioned him to be a musketeer."

"Shut up, Bobby," said Fritzy. "I think there's going to be a fight."

"Wow," whispered Keith. "This is kind of cool—"

"Shhhhh," hissed Bobby.

The large guard waved D'Artagnan away. "Go," he said nastily. "The King's Guard has no jurisdiction here."

The stranger inched closer to the boys. "When I tell you to duck, get down—fast." he whispered to them with authority.

"Is he kidding?" asked Keith.

"Just do as he says," commanded Bobby.

Swords waved through the air with great bravado. The Cardinal's Guards laughed and joked at the uneven odds. The stranger stood motionless behind the boys, his stare as hard and sharp as his sword.

"Well, stranger," laughed the large guard as he waved his plumed hat toward his companions. "Which of us do you choose to fight first?"

The man's steel gaze brightened. A smile split his narrow face.

"Oh," began the stranger brightly, "it would seem to be unfair odds to engage only one at a time. I think the three of you together might manage to give me a fight—"

"The devil!" exclaimed the large guard. "Why, you insolent dog!"

The handsome stranger raised a thinly-gloved hand and, with a flourish, waved it nonchalantly through the chilly night air. "On guard!" he cried. "Fight, or prepare to die!" Then to the boys, under his breath, he whispered, "Duck!"

Swords quickly flashed overhead as Bobby dropped to the cold cobblestone, pulling Fritzy and Keith along with him.

"What the—" began Fritzy before Bobby cut him off.

"Stay down!"

Thin, shiny blades sliced the night air above the huddled boys, as three swords came together as one against the stranger's blade. The sound of steel against steel echoed crisply along the empty street. The stranger leaped gracefully over the three friends, landing in a full lunge.

"Ouch!" cried one of the cardinal's guards. The boys were not sure which one. "My leg! The lunatic pierced my leg!"

The stranger laughed loudly as he waved his sword at the two remaining assailants. "To the bakery, my wee musketeers!" he shouted at the boys. "Xavier will watch over you!"

Bobby grabbed Fritzy and Keith and pointed toward the bakery's stained glass and wooden doorway.

"GO!" Bobby yelled. His friends scrambled across the cobblestones without looking back. Bobby glanced over his shoulder. The stranger and two of the guards were still locked in combat. The third guard lay writhing on the cold street, clutching his crimson wound.

"Only two left to fight?" cried the stranger as his blade slashed the air. The guards retreated from his masterful swordsmanship. The swordsman lowered his blade, glancing up and down the deserted street. "Surely there must be more of your comrades afoot. Fighting only two of the Cardinal's buffoons is far too easy."

"Who dares to address the Cardinal's Guard in such a manner?" shouted the large nosed guard, his sword still raised and pointed at his boasting opponent.

The stranger removed his hat with a flourish and bowed to the two waiting swordsman.

"My name is D'Artagnan, my large-nosed friend!" he exclaimed.

"D'Artagnan!" cried Bobby. He glanced over at his two friends huddled in the bakery doorway. "I told you he was D'Artagnan."

D'Artagnan looked over his shoulder. He shot Bobby a questioning glance. It was for only a second, but a second was all the large guard needed to strike. Sword raised, he rushed blindly at D'Artagnan.

"Look out!" cried Bobby pointing toward the guard's wild charge.

D'Artagnan turned quickly toward the adversary who was nearly on him. The young agile swordsman leaped backward just as the tip of the cardinal's guard's sword passed through the air exactly where D'Artagnan's chest had been only a second before. With a loud, brassy clank, D'Artagnan brought his blade down hard upon the man's sword breaking it cleanly in half. The unfortunate blade's top half echoed loudly as it hit the cold cobblestones.

The guard's face flushed noticeably as he drew away from D'Artagnan's blade.

"Ah, Monsieur," said D'Artagnan sarcastically. "It seems as if you have lost something—"

"You fiend!" replied the guard. Then, turning toward his companion he cried, "Get him!"

The third guard raised his sword and charged. It was to no avail; D'Artagnan's skill and cunning were far too much for the inferior swordsman. Back and forth they lunged and parried, their swords flashing brightly beneath the gaslights. D'Artagnan's eyes glowed with excitement.

Bobby pulled himself up from the street. The fight raged just in front of him.

"Get over here!" screamed Fritzy from the safety of the doorway.

"Hurry!" followed Keith.

As Bobby moved toward his friends, a large gloved hand grabbed him from behind. Bobby felt the glove's rough palm as it pressed against his mouth.

"At least I have *you*!" exclaimed the large guard.

"D'Artagnan!" yelled Fritzy. "He's got Bobby!"

D'Artagnan acknowledged Fritzy with a nod before intensifying the fight. But the guard was not to be denied his chance to defeat the superior swordsman and rallied with all his effort. The clash of swords was deafening.

Dragging Bobby down the street, the large guard's grip tightened over the boys mouth. Bobby managed to open his mouth just enough to allow one of the man's gloved fingers between his teeth. He bit down—hard!

"Owwww!" screamed the guard as he pulled his bitten hand from Bobby's mouth. "Why you little—"

Bobby swung around and with every ounce of his strength hit the guard in the stomach. The guard doubled over. Fritzy and Keith let out a loud cheer before running to Bobby's aid. The three boys beat at the guard's legs and body with their crude wooden swords, sending him running down the street into the darkness.

Meanwhile D'Artagnan moved across the cobblestones with incredible grace. He parried every attack that his opponent could conceive. The guard, whose shoulders were sagging, was exhausted and overmatched. Nevertheless, he took one last lunge. D'Artagnan easily avoided the misguided blade and disarmed his opponent, sending the blade crashing to the street.

"I am at your mercy," said the guard as he lowered his head.

D'Artagnan smiled. "Well, boys," he said brightly. "What do the fates have in store for our brave friend here?"

"What's that mean?" asked Keith, scratching at his short, black curls.

Fritzy sighed loudly.

"It means," began Bobby. "What should we do with him?"

"Oh," said Keith.

"Shall we let the scoundrel go?" asked D'Artagnan expressively.

The boys glanced at each other and shrugged.

"Or," continued D'Artagnan with narrowed eyes, "Shall

I skewer him upon the end of my blade—"

"No!" cried Bobby. "Please don't kill him."

D'Artagnan eyed Fritzy and Keith. "And you," he asked Fritzy. "Do you agree with your friend?"

"I don't know," replied Fritzy. "Tell me more about that skewer thing—" Bobby smacked Fritzy on the shoulder. "Ouch!"

Bobby eyed Fritzy impatiently before turning back to D'Artagnan. "Please don't kill him," he pleaded.

"Okay," said the frowning Fritzy. "Don't kill him. But, how about you make him bleed—just a little—?" Bobby let fly with another right, landing on the already bruised spot on Fritzy's shoulder. "Ouch!" cried Fritzy.

D'Artagnan chuckled before gazing at Keith. "And you?"

"N-N-No!"

D'Artagnan turned toward the guard and laughed out loud.

"Today is the luckiest of days for you, Monsieur," he said. "Your jury has agreed that you shall live this day." D'Artagnan rubbed his chin thoughtfully. "But," he continued, "there must be some type of punishment... Ah... I have it!"

D'Artagnan swiped his blade twice across the guard's midsection cutting the top of his trousers, making them drop into a heap below his knees.

"There is your punishment!" exclaimed D'Artagnan. "Now gather up your sword and your wounded comrade and leave this place—at once!"

As the two guards moved away, one limping and the

other tripping over his sagging trousers, the boys raised their wooden swords in triumph.

"All for one!" exclaimed Bobby.

"One for all!" Fritzy and Keith cried loudly.

Chapter Six
A Little Surprise

D'Artagnan stood motionless, his gaze fixed hard upon the three boys who waved their crude wooden swords overhead in celebration.

"Who are you?" he asked. "How do you know…?" D'Artagnan's voice trailed off.

"Uh, oh," said Bobby to his friends.

"What's wrong?" asked Fritzy.

"I think D'Artagnan was surprised to hear the 'all for one—one for all' thing coming from a bunch of kids he's never seen before," replied Bobby, before turning to the confused D'Artagnan. "Look, Mr. D'Artagnan, I can explain how we knew—"

"You must know, Monsieur Max, yes?" inquired D'Artagnan quickly interrupting Bobby. The Frenchman's eyes glowed with excitement.

"He's my grandfather—"

"I knew it!" exclaimed D'Artagnan. "Monsieur Max has told me all about you." He waved enthusiastically at Bobby. "You are Bobby, no?"

"Yes," Bobby replied brightly. "Grandpa Max told you about me?"

"Yes, yes," replied D'Artagnan. "And your friends, as well."

D'Artagnan glanced at Fritzy and Keith while rubbing his chin thoughtfully.

"You," he said pointing a finger at Fritzy, "must be Fritzy. Max told me about your funny, bowed legs."

Keith laughed loudly as Fritzy's face flushed.

"Shut up, Keith!" exclaimed the blushing Fritzy.

"And that leaves Keith," said D'Artagnan brightly. "Who, of course, I would know anywhere by his dark, curly hair."

Fritzy elbowed Keith in the ribs.

"Cut it out!"

"Yes, yes." D'Artagnan smiled. "All three of you are exactly as Monsieur Max has described. Come inside. Let us enjoy one of Xavier's creme puffs."

Keith clutched his stomach with both hands and groaned softly.

"What *is* this?" inquired D'Artagnan. "A boy who does not care for crème-puffs?"

Bobby laughed. "No," he said between chuckles. "I think Keith has already had enough of Xavier's crème-puffs."

D'Artagnan smiled and motioned toward the bakery door.

"One can never get enough of Xavier's pastries," he said brightly.

Xavier's crème-puffs paled in comparison to the wonderful chocolate cake that he happily placed in the center of the large round table nearest the blistering hot ovens. The boys and D'Artagnan gathered around Xavier's magnificent, gooey, three layer chocolate masterpiece. The baker quickly cut and served up three enormous pieces, each dripping with dark, thick icing.

"Wow!" exclaimed Keith, as Xavier pushed a plate holding the heavy, chocolate slab across the table. Keith grabbed a large chunk of cake with his fingers and stuffed it lovingly into his mouth. "Thif-if-da-bef-cay-ife-eva-ha!"

Xavier cocked his head. "What did he say?" he said to no one in particular.

"He said he likes your cake," replied Fritzy before shoving a handful into his own mouth.

"Thank you," said Xavier as he watched the two boys devour their luscious prize.

Bobby laughed at the sight of his friends' chocolate covered faces. Then, before taking a bite himself, Bobby glanced over toward D'Artagnan who stood near the oven. The swordsman looked troubled.

"What's wrong, D'Artagnan?" asked Bobby. "We won. Aren't you happy?"

D'Artagnan frowned. "I will only be happy when I find my companions."

"You mean Athos, Porthos and Aramis?"

"I am afraid so, my young friend. They have been

missing for days."

As Bobby gazed at the mountain of chocolate that Xavier had baked, he remembered something Grandpa Max had told him.

"Is it really my grandfather's fault?" Bobby asked.

D'Artagnan appeared startled. "But, whatever do you mean, Bobby?"

Bobby scratched at his head nervously. It was difficult for him to gather his thoughts while his two friends relentlessly devoured piece after piece of the chocolate cake. He wanted to laugh at their frosting smeared hands and faces but D'Artagnan seemed truly troubled.

"Well," said Bobby, "before we...uh...got here, Grandpa Max was going on and on about Athos, Porthos and Aramis being held prisoner by the Cardinal. He said that it was his fault."

D'Artagnan's frown turned up into a smile.

"I have to admit that you're grandfather has gotten into trouble more than once since he began to visit... but he cannot be blamed for the Cardinal's actions."

"Why is the Cardinal holding them?" Bobby asked.

D'Artagnan shook his head regrettably. "He knows of the mission her Majesty the Queen has asked me to undertake."

Bobby's eyes narrowed, "But how will you go to England to get the diamond studs from the Duke of Buckingham without Athos, Porthos and Aramis—"

"The devil!" cried D'Artagnan, his sharp, handsome features flushing red. "How could you possibly know this?" He began to pace. "No one knew of this plan but the Queen and myself. Even my friends knew nothing except the fact that they were to assist me in reaching London—"

The door burst open, abruptly silencing D'Artagnan. It was Grandpa Max!

"Grandpa!" exclaimed Bobby as he ran to greet him. Fritzy and Keith fell in behind him. Within moments, the three boys were all hugging Max tightly. Grandpa Max responded with an eager smile.

"You made it!" he cried happily. "I was hoping you boys would come."

"Max!" hollered Xavier with delight. "You look hungry. Sit and have some cake."

"Ah, Max," said D'Artagnan. "We need to talk."

"Grandpa," said a concerned Bobby. "Where have you been?"

"Did you find him?" inquired D'Artagnan.

"Not exactly," he replied with a smile.

"What does that mean?"

"What's going on, Grandpa?" Bobby asked worriedly. "Find who?"

Still smiling, Grandpa Max nodded before gently freeing himself from the boys' loving grasp. He moved to the door. It swung open slowly.

"May I introduce my new friend, Jeanne?"

Bobby's jaw dropped as the door opened fully, revealing the most beautiful girl he had ever seen. Her dark round eyes were set perfectly above two rosy cheeks, a button nose and thick full lips. Her face was framed by long brown curls, making Bobby's heart soar.

"What is this Max?" cried D'Artagnan. "Where is Monsieur Baudouin?"

Grandpa Max scratched his head. "It seems that our guide is being held at the Bastille. This young lady is his daughter."

"What? How can this be?"

Jeanne stepped into the shop. Bobby nearly gasped out loud.

"Because, monsieur," she said firmly, "someone informed the Cardinal of my father's plans to assist you."

"Sacré Bleu!" exclaimed D'Artagnan as he slammed his fist down on the table. "What are we to do?"

"I will show you the way," replied Jeanne.

"You!" D'Artagnan shook his head. "You are a girl!"

"But, monsieur—"

"It is too dangerous!"

Grandpa Max quickly stepped in. "D'Artagnan," he began, "you do not know the routes—"

"I *will* find my way," he replied. "I will not endanger the girl—"

"Jeanne," she quickly corrected.

"—Jeanne," said D'Artagnan.

"We have no choice," said Max, placing a comforting hand upon Jeanne's shoulder. "Who else will show us the way? You don't dare hire another guide, because the Cardinal would—"

D'Artagnan waved at Grandpa Max for silence.

"I know. I know," D'Artagnan said, with a disappointed shake of the head. "The Cardinal would find out, and arrest him as well."

"Grandpa," said Bobby. "What's going on?"

Max glanced toward D'Artagnan. The Frenchman nodded tersely.

"You see," began Grandpa Max, "Athos, Porthos and Aramis were to accompany D'Artagnan to London. The idea was that if one would fall, the others would continue on—"

"That's right!" exclaimed Bobby. "That way, at least one would reach Buckingham with the Queen's letter—"

"Shhhh!" hushed D'Artagnan. "The Cardinal's spies are everywhere…" He raised an eyebrow at Bobby. "How is it that you boys know so much about my mission? It is almost as if you know what is about to happen… as if you had read it in a book."

Bobby's eyes glanced at Keith and Fritzy before finally widening at Grandpa Max.

"To be sure, D'Artagnan," said Max, who smiled slyly as if to dismiss what Bobby had said. "The boy merely guessed—"

"I am not so convinced …" D'Artagnan shook his head before focusing on Jeanne. "You are certain you know the way?" he asked pointedly.

Jeanne nodded. "For what reason do we risk such a perilous journey?" she asked.

D'Artagnan sat near the fire and sighed. "The success of this journey may mean the difference between war and peace with England," he began. "The Queen of France and Duke of Buckingham in England are best friends. The King of France gave the Queen a precious gift of two diamond studs.

The Queen then gave these same diamond studs to her friend the Duke of Buckingham. Alas, the King will be furious if he found out she gave his gift to another.

Jeanne gasped. Grandpa Max and the boys pretended to be surprised.

"Somehow, the cardinal has found out about these studs and has convinced the King to have the Queen wear them at the ballet."

"But Monsieur," said Jeanne. "How can the Queen wear what she does not have?"

D'Artagnan grinned. "That is exactly the problem," he said brightly. "The Queen has asked me to go to Buckingham and retrieve the studs and bring them back in time for the ballet."

"Sacre Bleu!" exclaimed Jeanne. "What if the Queen does not wear the studs?"

D'Artagnan stared blankly into the crackling fire. "I do not know for sure," he said softly, "but I can guess. There will be war with England."

Jeanne popped up and pushed her fists firmly against her hips.

"Then we have no choice," she began, "but to go to England."

D'Artagnan swung one leg onto a chair and spread his arms out wide.

"Well, Max," he said brightly. "If I must, I must. But," he added emphatically, "I cannot travel alone with a young girl. You will accompany us and we shall act as a family."

"But…D'Artagnan, I must protest," replied Grandpa

Max. "I have the boys to look after—"

"We're goin'!" shouted Bobby.

"What?" cried Fritzy and Keith together.

Bobby turned toward his friends.

"Don't you see," he began excitedly. "This is what *we* wanted—to be the three musketeers—to have a D'Artagnan!"

"You're crazy!" exclaimed Keith.

"Wait," said Fritzy. He walked over to Bobby and stood by his side. "Bobby's right. We can't pass this up—"

"But, my mom said to be home by five," whined Keith.

"He's right, Grandpa," said Bobby.

"Not to worry, boys." Max smiled broadly. "I'll take care of everything." The old man shot the boys a sly wink. "So, my little musketeers, what do you say?"

The boys brought their wooden swords together over their heads.

"All for one—one for all!" they exclaimed enthusiastically.

Bobby glanced at the smiling D'Artagnan.

"Well then," said the swordsman, "it seems that our little family has just gotten bigger."

Chapter Seven
The Real Musketeers

"**B**ah!" snapped Porthos as his thick hand rattled the door handle for the tenth time. "I feel like a trapped rat!" he declared before planting his ample frame into a chair near the door.

"Relax, my old friend," said the calming voice of Athos. "There is plenty of food and wine. Enjoy!"

"What of D'Artagnan?" growled Porthos, while still staring at the locked door. Then he pointed impatiently at Aramis, who sat quietly studying a chess board. "How can he play chess at a time like this?"

Aramis glanced at his two companions. Then, with a short sigh, went back to studying the game.

Athos rose from the table and poured his companion a fresh glass of Spanish wine.

"D'Artagnan can take care of himself." Athos held the lip of the dark bottle of wine over a third, long stemmed glass.

"Aramis?"

Aramis drew his eyes from the chessboard and shook his head.

"If it were not for that old man," groused Porthos.

"True," said Athos before bringing the wine to his lips.

"What was his name again?"

"I believe it was Max—"

"That is it!" exclaimed Porthos. "If not for him, we would be with D'Artagnan now."

"Aye!" agreed Athos.

"No!" snapped Aramis, who turned his attention away from the chessboard once again. "It was not Max's fault! We've gotten *ourselves* into this mess!"

"But, Aramis—"

"No, Porthos!" exclaimed Aramis, quickly interrupting his companion. "Max was only doing what D'Artagnan asked him to do. How was he to know he was being followed?"

"I know." Porthos stood, his fists clenched tightly. "If I could just open *that* door—"

"Then what, my large friend," said Aramis. "We were brought here blindfolded. For all we know, they might have taken us to England."

"The devil!" growled Porthos.

"Now, please sit down and have some wine—"

Aramis was suddenly interrupted by the sound of muffled voices. Like a cat, his eyes scanned the room.

"What is it?" inquired Athos upon observing his friend's odd behavior.

"Shhhhh!" hissed Aramis, as he crept silently toward

the idle fireplace. "Come," he whispered. Aramis waved his friends closer.

The muffled voices grew louder.

"It's definitely a man," said Aramis as he pushed his head further into the cold fireplace.

"Richelieu?" inquired Athos.

"Maybe…ahhh…" said Aramis. A sly smile spread across his face "… and a woman as well."

"What are they saying?" asked Porthos.

"Shhhh," Aramis hissed once more. "I cannot hear if you will not be quiet!"

The three imprisoned musketeers huddled tensely before the open hearth, hoping for the muffled voices to move closer to the fireplace above. It wasn't more than a moment before they did. The two voices echoed up the stack, but were clear enough to hear.

"You know him best, Athos," whispered Aramis. "Is it indeed, the Cardinal?"

Athos nodded.

"And the woman?"

Athos narrowed his eyes and concentrated greatly on the woman's voice. After another moment, the musketeer's face drained of color.

"What is wrong?" inquired Porthos.

"You recognize the woman?" Aramis pressed his friend.

Athos did not reply.

Aramis shot Porthos a questionable glance before turning his attention back to the fireplace. The musketeers stood quietly listening intently to the devilish plot developing above.

Cardinal Richelieu was indeed planning to thwart D'Artagnan's mission to England and this unknown woman was to be the tool to do so. The woman was to arrange for her agents to lay in wait along the path to the docks that would take D'Artagnan across the English Channel.

"NO!" cried Porthos.

"Shhhh!" hissed Aramis. "If we can hear them—they can hear us," he whispered.

Porthos held a finger to his lips.

"You will see to it, Lady de Winter," said the voice of the Cardinal.

"Yes, Your Eminence," replied the woman. "Your plan will be carried out."

"Under no circumstances must those jewels reach the Queen," continued the Cardinal.

"I assure you D'Artagnan will fail," said Lady de Winter, quick to reassure Richelieu.

The voices suddenly grew distant and muffled as the cardinal and Lady de Winter moved away from the fireplace.

"Aramis!" cried Porthos in a harsh whisper. "We must get to D'Artagnan!"

"Aye," replied Aramis. "Athos," he called urgently. Athos, without any doubt, had always been the leader of this small band of friends. As in all other times of crises, Aramis and Porthos turned to him.

Athos remained silent. He poured himself another glass of Spanish wine.

"This is no time for wine!" shouted Porthos. "We must

escape!"

Athos appeared troubled. His full, handsome face had taken on a sullen uncomfortable look. Athos thoughtfully twisted the end of his mustache.

"I believe there is something wrong with Athos," said Porthos.

Aramis nodded then joined Athos at the table.

"So, my friend," said Aramis, as he tipped what was left of the bottle into Athos' empty glass. "Is Porthos right? Is there something wrong? You know this woman?"

Athos threw back his head and emptied the glass. He nodded.

"I am afraid that I do know her," he said absently. "She was my wife!"

"What?" cried Aramis.

"What!" echoed Porthos.

"But," Athos continued softly. "That does not matter. Please, my friends, do not ask me of her again for I cannot say why His Eminence called her Lady de Winter. All that matters is that we escape from our well stocked prison so we may warn D'Artagnan of her treachery." He turned to his companions, arm extended. "All for one!"

Aramis and Porthos eagerly placed their hands upon his.

"One for all," they cried.

Chapter Eight
Grandpa Max

"**W**ell then," announced D'Artagnan. "I guess we had all better get some sleep."

"But D'Artagnan," said Bobby. "What about the Cardinal's guards? What if they come back?"

D'Artagnan smiled and pointed a thumb over his shoulder at Xavier.

"I think I can help with that," said the baker slyly. "Come, everyone into the back room."

"Not the one we came out of?" inquired Fritzy.

"Exactly," replied Xavier.

"But won't they find us?" asked Keith.

Xavier stepped to the door and opened it with a flourish. "We shall see."

One by one, the boys, Grandpa Max and Jeanne followed the baker through the dark doorway. Xavier lit a long, thin candle. It slowly flooded the space with a dim, flickering light. The pudgy baker took one last look into the bakery before closing the door behind D'Artagnan.

"Come." Xavier scurried to the front of the group, beckoning them to follow.

Holding the candle out to light the way, Xavier walked slowly across the rough wooden floor. The thin, flickering flame caused shadows to dance along the inky darkness.

"Where are we going, Grandpa Max?" inquired Bobby.

"You'll see," he replied.

Xavier stopped in front of a large cabinet of shelves near the back wall and handed D'Artagnan the candle. Then, cautioning everyone to stand back, the baker put his shoulder up against the side of the cabinet and pushed. Xavier let out a grunt. The case moved slowly and noiselessly along the floor. It revealed a dark, rectangular opening.

Bobby, Fritzy and Keith stepped up to the edge and stared into the darkness.

A cold chill ran up Bobby's spine. "What's down there?"

Xavier snatched the candle from D'Artagnan and stepped into the opening.

"You see," said the baker cheerfully. "There are stairs."

"B-but, where do they lead?" inquired Fritzy.

"Why, to the cellar," replied Xavier. "Where else?"

Jeanne joined the boys near the edge. She gasped loudly as she peered into the mysterious hole in the floor.

"Please do not worry, my little ones," said Xavier, rushing to reassure them. "You will be safe down there—safe from the guards."

"I'm not goin' down there!" exclaimed Fritzy.

"I'm with Fritzy!" cried Keith. "No way!"

Bobby reached for Grandpa Max, quickly finding the old man's bony, but familiar, hand. He looked into his grandfather's twinkling eyes. There was no doubt that Bobby's grandfather was thoroughly enjoying every moment of their adventure. The old man's eyes met his grandson's. Only a half smile and a nod were needed to reassure Bobby that everything would be okay.

"The guards will be back," said Xavier. "And they will search every shop and alley."

"Then, if it's not safe up here," said Bobby, mustering up all the courage he could. "We'd better go down there!"

"What?" cried Fritzy.

"Are you crazy?" snapped Keith.

"Ah… Bobby," sighed D'Artagnan. "You have the bravery expected of a musketeer."

Bobby nodded to D'Artagnan before turning to his friends. "Look guys," he began, "it's only for tonight. Right, D'Artagnan?"

"Oui."

"See. One night—"

"I-I am not afraid," said Jeanne. The pitch in her voice betrayed her false bravado.

"See," said Bobby. "Even Jeanne's not afraid."

Fritzy and Keith glanced over the edge once more. Fritzy smiled and Keith shrugged his shoulders before turning to Bobby.

"Okay, Bobby," said Fritzy. "You first!"

"Yeah, Mr. *Brave Musketeer*," Keith happily added. "You go first."

Bobby gulped loudly. He took another look down the dark stairwell then glanced over his shoulder at D'Artagnan. The Gascon gave Bobby a smile and the same reassuring nod as Grandpa Max.

"Come quickly, all of you," said Xavier as he headed down the steps. "Quickly, before the guards return."

"C'mon, guys," Bobby said bravely, as he followed the baker down the stairs. "Follow me!"

Bobby followed Xavier and the flickering candle down the dark, wooden stairway. The old stairs strained against their weight, squeaking loudly with every step. Fritzy and Keith were close on Bobby's heels. So close, that more than once, one or the other bumped up against his back. Grandpa Max assisted Jeanne down the narrow steps with D'Artagnan guarding the rear.

Surprisingly, the room below appeared clean and well kept. As Xavier lit two tall oil lamps, their growing flames brought the entire room into view. The ceiling was low and the floor was hardened dirt. Except for some dampness, the air seemed clean. Several small tables filled the center of the room surrounded by five crude, wooden bunks.

"There are enough beds and bedding here for all," said Xavier, while opening the door of what appeared to be large cabinet. He looked at Jeanne. "Mademoiselle," he continued, "you will sleep in here. Do not worry; it is another hidden room."

Xavier took Jeanne by the arm and led her toward the small doorway. "A young lady must have her privacy."

"Wow, Xavier," said Fritzy. "This place is really cool."

"Cool?" inquired the baker. "Do you need a jacket, or maybe a blanket?"

"No, no," replied the smiling boy. "I meant this place is really neat!"

"Oh, thank you," said Xavier proudly. "I do clean often—"

The boys started to laugh.

"What is so funny?" inquired Xavier.

"I'll try to explain later," replied Bobby.

Xavier frowned. "In that case, make yourselves comfortable," he began, the corner of his mouth returning to a smile. "I will bring down some food shortly before you go to bed."

"What is this place?" inquired Bobby.

"A place to hide the Cardinal's enemies," replied Xavier.

"Why?"

"Cardinal Richelieu's powers nearly match King Louis' himself," began the baker. His tone turned quite serious. "The Cardinal has made many enemies of those who would support the king, including His Majesty's Musketeers. So, my little musketeers, Xavier will hide those who the Cardinal, most assuredly, would banish unjustly to the Bastille."

"Paris is a most dangerous place these days," added D'Artagnan. "The Cardinal's spies are everywhere."

"Uh…Xavier," said Keith softly. "What if we have to… you know… go?"

"Go?"

"Yeah…you know…go?"

"Ah," said the baker with a laugh. "You see that door over there? It leads to the toilet."

"Great!" exclaimed Keith as he rushed through the small wooden doorway. A few moments passed before he stumbled back into the room. "There are just some closets with big bowls in them."

"Oui…toilets."

"Oh brother," hissed Keith as he turned and went back through the doorway.

The small band gathered around the three tables in the center of the room. Xavier had supplied a light snack for everyone before bed. Aside from Fritzy and Keith's bothersome clowning, the meal passed with very little conversation.

Finally, D'Artagnan said, "You know my little musketeers… and Mademoiselle. This journey could prove to be most dangerous. I cannot guarantee your safety."

Bobby gulped down his last bite of food. "Don't worry about us, Mr. D'Artagnan."

"But, I must," replied D'Artagnan.

"We'll be okay," added Fritzy. "Heck, we're Musketeers too—"

"Shush!" hissed D'Artagnan, holding a finger to his pursed lips.

"What is it?" whispered Grandpa Max.

The Frenchman did not reply, his finger simply pointed up. Five sets of curious eyes followed that digit. The air hung still. No one dared to breathe. The sound of boots banging against the floor above them echoed through their small chamber. The Cardinal's men had returned.

The footsteps grew louder and louder as they drew closer to the hidden stairway. Muffled voices echoed overhead. The sound of Xavier's friendly, robust voice was by far the loudest. Sword in hand, D'Artagnan crept quietly to the staircase ready to do battle if necessary. The boys followed suit, their broad wooden swords drawn and ready. For a brief moment, D'Artagnan's glance strayed from the ceiling just long enough to give the boys a smile.

The voices sounded as if they came from directly over the stairway. D'Artagnan placed one foot onto the steps. Bobby froze, barely able to breathe. Fritzy stood motionless—still as a statue. Keith's face blanched and his upper lip was covered with sweat.

"You see, they do not hide in Xavier's back room," said the baker's muffled voice. "I would have for sure seen them for I have been busy baking all evening long."

"Are there any other rooms?" inquired the equally muffled voice of a guard.

"Monsieur," replied Xavier. "As you can see, there is only one way out of the backroom, through the kitchen. There is not so much as a window or even a crack big enough for a mouse. No one could possibly get in or out without my knowing."

Then the footsteps moved away, cautiously stopping from time to time before they disappeared into the bakery. D'Artagnan sheathed his sword and sat breathlessly on a step. Everyone, including Grandpa Max and Jeanne, smiled at each other. They were safe—for now.

Bobby tossed in his bunk. He couldn't sleep. More than Fritzy's long winded snoring; the excitement of their adventure kept him awake. Bobby was living his dream—to be a King's Musketeer. Here they were, in old Paris, hiding from the Cardinal's guards with none other than D'Artagnan, one of the greatest characters in the history of literature.

Keith's rapid-fire snores suddenly joined Fritzy's. Now he was surrounded. With snores pouring from his two friends' opened, drooling mouths, Bobby had to move. Quietly, trying not to disturb anyone, he pulled his blanket from the crude, bundled straw mattress and sought out a quieter area so he might get some sleep. As Bobby tiptoed past Grandpa Max's bunk, he heard a soft hiss. He stopped. It was his grandfather whispering his name.

"Bobby."

Bobby moved closer to Grandpa Max's bunk.

"Grandpa," he whispered back softly.

"Come and sit a minute." Max whispered so gently that Bobby could hardly hear what he said.

Bobby sat on the edge of Grandpa Max's bunk. "Is this all really happening?" he asked.

His grandfather nodded.

"How can it be?" asked Bobby. "It's gotta be impossible!"

Grandpa Max held a silencing finger up to his lips.

Bobby sighed.

"I'm really not sure how," began his grandfather, "but it would seem that the closet and my apartment hold some strange power."

"But, Grandpa," whispered Bobby, "Dad built that apartment—"

"I know, I know. But there must be something about…" Max scratched his pointy chin. "… Wait a minute," he said so excitedly that Bobby thought he would wake everyone.

"Shush, Grandpa."

"No, no," he said, whispering softly once again. "I just realized something." Max shot up and grabbed Bobby by the shoulders. "The books, Bobby, the books!"

"What about the books?"

"Don't you remember? A few months ago I went to an old, old house for an estate sale. The agent said that there were lots of old books. You know… the classics."

"Now that you mention it…"

"Well," Grandpa Max continued, "I remember there was this older woman, she had to be nearly a hundred years old, selling all of these wonderful old books." Max was sitting up on the bunk's narrow edge. "From the moment I walked into the room, I realized the woman was staring at me. Her eyes followed me everywhere. I remember it made me feel very uncomfortable. Quickly, I picked out a few books and paid her. I just wanted to get out of there. Then…"

"Then, what?"

"Then when I turned to leave, she grabbed my arm. When I stopped to see what she wanted, the woman went behind the desk and picked up a small box and handed it to me. I looked inside. There were a handful of old leather bound volumes—"

"You mean like, *The Three Musketeers, The Hound of*

the Baskervilles and *Robin Hood*?"

"Yes, yes," replied Max.

"How—?"

"I don't know. But, I do remember that when I went to pay for the books, the woman wouldn't take any money. She said that the books belonged to me."

"Wow," hissed Bobby.

"It *must* be the books," said Grandpa Max, "but how?"

Chapter Nine
Ambuscade

The morning light streamed brightly through the front windows as the sleepy guests meandered into the bakery. The long night spent in the dark cellar made the light from the sun-filled bakery explode into everyone's eyes. Bobby rubbed his eyes. They stung from the brightness. Fritzy yawned loudly as he shuffled behind the flour covered Xavier. Keith sat down, cleared a spot at the table and laid his head down.

"I trust everyone slept well," Xavier said brightly. "Breakfast?"

"I'm too tired to eat," replied Fritzy. "I didn't sleep a wink."

"You're too tired?" snapped Bobby. "Your snoring kept me up half the night."

"Quiet!" hissed Keith without moving his lips. "I'm trying to sleep."

"You too?" cried Bobby jabbing his thumb over his

shoulder at Fritzy. "You snored louder than he did!"

"Now, now, boys," said Grandpa Max. "No more fighting."

D'Artagnan covered his mouth, but everyone knew he was quietly laughing.

"Ahhh," he snorted. "The boys sound more like Athos, Porthos and Aramis than *they* do themselves."

"They argue, too?" asked Bobby.

"More than you could possibly know."

"But, the book…"

D'Artagnan shot Bobby a sideways glance. "Book, what book?"

Grandpa Max quickly interrupted. "I'm starving," he said while rubbing his wiry midsection. "How about something to eat, Xavier?"

"But, of course," replied the jolly baker. "Please be seated. The pastries are nearly ready."

Xavier spread out a breakfast fit for a king. Every type of pastry Bobby, Fritzy and Keith could ever imagine lay before their eager eyes. Donuts, pastries and cakes of all sizes and shapes littered the table.

"Wow!" cried Keith and Fritzy in unison.

Bobby laughed. "I thought you guys were too tired to eat?"

Keith shook his head. "That's when I thought we were having more cream puffs."

"Yeah!" exclaimed Fritzy before attacking the pastries with both hands.

Breakfast passed quickly and quietly. The boys wasted

no time in sampling each and every one of Xavier's wonderful pastries. D'Artagnan and Grandpa Max sipped thoughtfully at cups of thick, steaming coffee. Bobby's grandpa occasionally glanced toward the boys, who were eating with great relish. Bobby noticed that Jeanne had hardly touched the cream filled éclair Xavier had prepared especially for her.

Bobby slid down the bench, closer to Jeanne. "What's wrong?" he asked after gulping down a bite of chocolate cake. "Aren't you hungry?"

Jeanne didn't answer. She just stared blankly at the éclair. Her face was sullen and pale.

Bobby didn't give up easily. "Would you like something else?" he asked.

Jeanne pulled her stare up from the table. Her large eyes set firmly on Bobby's.

"I am worried about my father," she said with a sigh in her voice. "I'm afraid that my father will be in the Bastille forever."

Now it was Bobby's turn to be silent. Because he didn't know what to say he looked away. Suddenly, a smile spread across his young face.

"Maybe D'Artagnan can save him!"

"Yeah!" cried Fritzy. "You and the Musketeers can save Jeanne's father, right D'Artagnan?"

At first, D'Artagnan frowned. "Hmmm," he began thoughtfully. Then a huge smile appeared below his neatly cut mustache. "Of course we will! First we go to Buckingham, then we save your father."

"How?" the girl asked hopefully.

"Uh…I'm not yet sure, my little mademoiselle," he replied. "But, mark my words, after the mission your father will be a free man."

"Oh, Monsieur D'Artagnan!" cried Jeanne as she rushed around the table and gave him a big hug. "You are indeed, my hero."

Bobby frowned. "Geez," he said softly thinking no one would hear. "It was my idea—"

Fritzy reached over and punched Bobby in the upper arm.

"Ow! What was that for?"

"You're jealous of D'Artagnan," Fritzy said playfully.

"Am not," scolded Bobby through clenched teeth.

"Are too," added Keith.

Bobby's face flushed crimson before wrestling Fritzy and Keith to the floor. The boys rolled across the kitchen, arms and legs flapping wildly in the air. Food flew in every direction to the sounds of boyish grunts and groans.

"Take it back!" cried Bobby as he ground a piece of gooey chocolate cake into Fritzy's already powdered sugar covered face.

Keith climbed onto the top of the pile and tried to pull his two friends apart.

"Will not!" replied the laughing Fritzy. "Your jealou—"

The big chunk of chocolate cake had finally found its mark; Bobby had managed to shove it into Fritzy's mouth.

"Now take it back!" cried Bobby.

Keith finally managed to separate his friends.

"Wow," said Fritzy popping up from the floor, wearing

a big chocolate smile. "That cake is great, Xavier. Is there any more?"

"Ah, yes," replied the baker with a smile. "But only if you stop fighting."

"I'll do anything for a piece of that cake."

"Me too," said Keith.

Bobby just sat on the floor and frowned.

Jeanne looked at Bobby disapprovingly and said, "*Boys.*"

Once the playful shoving and expected taunts stopped, the boys returned to their seats. D'Artagnan, who had been laughing at the boys' antics, had suddenly turned very serious.

"It is time to start our mission," he began softly. Xavier poured more of the thick coffee into his waiting cup. "First," he continued after taking a long sip. "I must go to my rooms. We will need money to complete the journey and I have more than enough hidden there."

"Can we go, too?" pleaded Bobby.

"Yeah, can we?" added Keith.

Fritzy couldn't speak. His mouth was jammed full of Xavier's wonderful chocolate cake.

D'Artagnan glanced at Grandpa Max.

"I see no reason why not," said Max replying to D'Artagnan's inquisitive look. "As long as you do as I tell you and stay out of sight of the guards."

"There are ways to get to my rooms that the Cardinal's guards would never think of traveling. It is easy to blend in among the alleys and markets of Paris."

"Then we can go?" inquired Bobby excitedly.

D'Artagnan reached across the table and touched the King's Musketeers white cross insignia that adorned the front of Bobby's homemade costume.

"Xavier," said the Gascon thoughtfully. "What do you say we make these lads look like little beggars?"

"But, of course," replied the baker. "When I have finished, even Grandpa Max won't recognize them."

"All right!" shouted Bobby and Keith.

"Aw wite!" echoed Fritzy through a delicious mouthful of cake.

The morning shadows disappeared as the midday sun moved gracefully over the cobblestone streets of Paris. D'Artagnan led the way. Bobby, Fritzy and Keith struggled to keep up with the Frenchman's much longer stride. The streets appeared quiet for the noon hour. With snorting steeds clip-clopping ahead, an occasional carriage filled the street with a racket loud enough to drown out the sound of store owners and vendors selling their wares to passersby.

Everything in the marketplace, especially the smells and sounds, seemed *so* foreign to Bobby and his friends. For three modern Midwestern kids this was quite an adventure. Fritzy tugged at Bobby's sleeve.

"Are we really doin' this or am I dreamin'?" he asked.

"Don't ask me," replied Bobby.

"I mean, here we are in old Paris, and everyone speaks English."

"Yeah, Bobby," said Keith. "How come everyone understands us?"

"Dunno," replied Bobby. "I'll ask D'Artagnan."

Bobby scurried along the uneven stone walkway, finally catching up with D'Artagnan.

"Hey D'Artagnan," he said breathlessly. "How come you guys all speak English?"

The swordsman narrowed his eyes and frowned.

"I do not understand," he replied.

"You know... Xavier, Jeanne and the bad guys. They all spoke English."

"No, no, my little friend," said D'Artagnan suspiciously. "No one spoke English."

Bobby scratched his head and gave his friends, who had just caught up, a shrug.

"Then how do you understand us?"

D'Artagnan stopped quickly. "Of course I can understand you, you are speaking French."

The boys shot each other a questioning glance.

"What's he talking about?" asked Fritzy.

"I don't know French," hissed Keith.

D'Artagnan waved his arms impatiently before starting back down the street. "Come, we must go."

Bobby scratched nervously at the ragged shirt covering his chest.

"Geez, D'Artagnan," he said softly. "Where did Xavier find these clothes, in the garbage?"

D'Artagnan looked back at the three rag covered boys and smiled. "Oui."

"Yew!" exclaimed Fritzy. "I knew I smelled something bad. I just thought it was Keith."

"Hey!" cried Keith while giving his friend a playful shove.

Bobby quickly stepped between them.

"These old clothes itch," said Bobby, as he scratched impatiently at his armpit.

Fritzy scrunched up his nose. "And smell."

"Quiet, my little musketeers. We are almost there," said D'Artagnan before quickly ducking down a narrow alley. "Come—this way!"

The boys followed obediently into the dark, narrow alleyway. It was deserted. Filthy wooden garbage bins lined the puddle covered, cobbled walkway. The musky smell of animals and rotted food burnt Bobby's nose.

D'Artagnan stopped quickly, extending his arms to keep the boys from rushing past. The Frenchman didn't utter a sound; the boys felt breathless with anticipation.

D'Artagnan's right hand moved slowly toward the handle of his sword.

"Something is not right here, my little musketeers," he whispered. "Let us go back to the street."

"What is it?" asked Bobby.

"No people," replied D'Artagnan, who urged Bobby and the others to start moving back. "There are always people in the alley. Something has scared them away. Be aware; I believe there is no good afoot."

Bobby felt an enormous lump in his throat. He glanced at Fritzy and Keith, who both appeared to be suffering from the same problem. His friends were as pale as ghosts. Bobby could only imagine what his own face looked like. He couldn't wait to get back to the sun filled street.

"Turn around and head back," said D'Artagnan, whose gaze was still fixed down the alley. "I will cover our retreat."

Without a word, the boys turned on their heels and started back toward the street. Too late! The path was blocked by three of the largest men the eleven-year-old boys could ever imagine. Dressed in the smart, red and black uniforms of the Cardinal's Guard, their smiling faces stared down the blades of three gleaming swords. Swords pointed directly at Bobby and his friends.

"Uh…D'Artagnan," squeaked Bobby, who felt as if he were about to faint.

"Not now, my little musketeer," snapped D'Artagnan.

"Uh…D'Artagnan," echoed Fritzy's trembling voice. "I-I think you should t-t-turn around."

"What is it—?" growled D'Artagnan as he spun towards the boys.

"The devil! Ambuscade!"

Chapter Ten
The Wee Musketeers

The boys stood frozen beneath the large shadowy figures. Bobby glanced back at D'Artagnan who, with sword neatly drawn, stood poised and ready for action.

"Surrender!" barked the tall guard. It was the man with the bulbous nose from the night before. Bobby felt his body shiver at the sound of his voice.

"Never!" spat D'Artagnan.

"Seize the boys!" cried the guard to his companions.

The large guard rushed toward Bobby. Within seconds, the boy felt a big, gloved hand wrap painfully around his throat. He squirmed helplessly within the man's iron grip. Bobby managed to turn his head slightly, only to see that his friends had met a similar fate.

"Hey," shouted Fritzy, "leggo!"

"Let go of me!" echoed Keith.

Bobby couldn't speak; the guard's grip was far too tight.

D'Artagnan lunged toward the guards. The large guard raised his hand in warning.

"One more step," croaked the guard through tightly clenched teeth, "and I will break this little one's neck."

D'Artagnan stopped fast. The guard smiled triumphantly at his companions before looking back to D'Artagnan.

"I command you to drop your sword and accompany us." The guard pulled Bobby closer. "The Cardinal wishes an audience."

"Don't do it—" cried Fritzy before the guard's meaty fist choked off his words.

D'Artagnan's cold stare softened and Bobby could swear the Frenchman was beginning to smile.

"You do not believe I will do it?" snarled the large guard.

Bobby gasped desperately for air.

D'Artagnan rested his blade casually against his shoulder. "Oh," he began, "indeed I do."

"Then drop your sword!"

"When you let the boys go."

The guards laughed loudly. Bobby had never felt fear like this. Deep, deep fear spread through his soul as the guard's fist tightened around his throat. *What is D'Artagnan doing*, he thought.

"Drop the sword, D'Artagnan, or the boy will die!"

D'Artagnan's smile broadened and his handsome eyes

brightened.

"What is so fun—?"

The guard never finished. A loud crash echoed through the alley. Bobby felt the guard's grip fall away. His lungs greedily filled with air as he fell onto the damp stones. Another crash echoed around them—and the second guard fell to the ground freeing Fritzy.

In an instant, D'Artagnan was on the third guard, who instantly released Keith. Blades flashed like bolts of lightning in the shaded alley. Bobby searched for his friends. Fritzy and Keith were on the ground but they looked as if they were all right.

Bobby jumped to his feet just as the guard who had been holding him pulled himself up to his knees. Bam! The guard hit the alley with a loud thump.

"Grandpa Max!" cried Bobby.

Bam! Grandpa Max let the guard have it one more time.

"In person!" he shouted. Grandpa Max was holding the top of one of the wooden trash bins. He beamed at his grandson. "Are you okay, Bobby?"

Bobby rubbed his throat thoughtfully. "I think so— D'Artagnan! Look out!"

The second guard that Grandpa Max had hit was up with sword drawn. He headed toward D'Artagnan who was still engaged with the third guard. Bobby had never seen swords flash so quickly. This guard seemed more than a match for D'Artagnan.

Bobby snatched the wooden bin cover from his grandfather's unsuspecting grip and stepped between the guard and D'Artagnan, who were still locked in a struggle.

"Out of my way, pipsqueak!" growled the guard. Bobby didn't budge. "Well then, you shall taste my steel!" The guard thrust the point of his long narrow blade at Bobby, who quickly held the wooden trash cover between himself and the blade's lethal tip. It stuck! No matter how hard the guard struggled to pull the blade from the wood, it would not come free.

The guard snarled as he continued the struggle.

Bobby held onto the trash bin cover with all of his might. "C'mon, guys!" he yelled. Fritzy and Keith jumped to their feet and ran toward the guard, screaming at the top of their lungs.

Fritzy wrapped himself around the guard's left leg as Keith tangled up the right. Bobby pushed against the trash bin cover with every ounce of his strength.

"Oof," went the guard, as Bobby rammed the handle of the sword into his assailant's stomach. "Let go of me!" he screamed as Fritzy and Keith each tightened their grip on his legs. Bobby yanked at the wooden bin cover, pulling the sword from the guard's unsuspecting hand.

"Grandpa Max!" cried Bobby, before tossing the wooden bin-cover and the sword to his grandfather. "Go help D'Artagnan! We've got this guy!"

Grandpa Max stood on the bin cover unsuccessfully attempting to pull the sword free.

Meanwhile, D'Artagnan had finally gotten the best of the third guard by backing him up against a tiny doorway.

"Surrender!" his cry echoed down the alley.

"Never!" growled the guard.

With a mighty swing of the blade, D'Artagnan disarmed his opponent. The guard's sword rattled against the alley's cold stones.

Fritzy and Keith maneuvered behind the second guard's legs as Bobby ran headlong into his midsection. With a great thud, the guard lay unconscious at the boys' feet.

With D'Artagnan disarming his guard, Grandpa Max still struggling with the sword and the boys celebrating their victory, no one noticed the large guard getting to his feet. Slowly, he crept toward Grandpa Max. Closer and closer he moved, until his gleaming sword was only inches from its mark.

"MAX!" cried a voice from the end of the alley. It was Jeanne. "LOOK OUT!"

As Grandpa Max swung around looking for Jeanne, he flung the sword over his shoulder. When he did, the wooden bin cover smacked the large guard right in the nose, knocking him to his knees. Crimson poured from the man's bulbous snout.

"Oh my," gasped Grandpa Max. "Did I do that?"

"Hey!" yelled Fritzy pointing toward the bleeding guard. "It's the guy from last night!"

D'Artagnan grabbed his guard by the arm and dragged him to the center of the alley.

"Ah, yes," he said brightly. "I recognize the nose."

"What has that old man done!" cried the large guard as he tried to stop the bleeding with his sleeve. "Look at my nose!"

"No thanks," said Fritzy.

"Gross!" exclaimed Keith.

"What should we do?" asked Bobby.

"There is some cord over there, boys," said D'Artagnan, pointing toward a long length of rope draped over a stair railing.

Fritzy and Keith snatched the rope. The boys and Grandpa Max began to tie up the guards.

"You are very brave boys," said D'Artagnan.

"Just like the Three Musketeers?" asked Fritzy.

D'Artagnan smiled. "No, my little ones, more like the Wee Musketeers!"

"Come," said D'Artagnan. "We have been detained long enough. My apartment is very close." Entering his sparsely furnished and cramped quarters, D'Artagnan ushered everyone inside and quickly shut the door.

"Why did you leave the bakery, Max?" inquired D'Artagnan.

"It was no longer safe," he replied. "I feared for Xavier. The guards were everywhere and I didn't want them to find us there. I'm not sure how we were able to get away."

"It is quite fortuitous for us that you did. Why didn't Xavier hide you in the basement like last night?"

"He would have, but the trap door jammed and we could not get down there. The guards were going shop to shop, house to house—"

"But still you escaped…hmm."

Bobby tugged at D'Artagnan's blousy sleeve. "Do you think the guards *let* Grandpa Max and Jeanne escape?"

D'Artagnan rubbed his chin. "Stay here," he began, "I

will return in a few moments. I must find Planchet."

"Your lackey?" inquired Bobby.

"Why yes," replied D'Artagnan. Then, narrowing one eye, he replied, "How did you know that?"

"Know what?"

"That Planchet was my lackey."

"I…uh…"

Grandpa Max quickly interrupted. "I must have mentioned that Planchet was your manservant," he said. "Right boys?"

Bobby gave his friends a nudge. Fritzy and Keith shot each other a quick glance.

"Oh yeah," said Fritzy. "Grandpa Max told us all about Planchet."

"Sure did," said Keith through a forced, toothy smile.

Grandpa Max took D'Artagnan by the arm and pushed him toward the door.

"There is no time to waste, D'Artagnan," he snapped. "Quickly…go find Planchet!"

D'Artagnan took one more thoughtful look at the boys. "I will return shortly. All of you stay out of sight!" In a flash, he disappeared behind the door as it slammed shut behind him.

Bobby let out a long breath. "Whew, that was a close one."

"Do you think he's getting suspicious, Grandpa Max?" asked Fritzy.

"I'm not sure. We'd best be more careful."

Jeanne stared incredulously from Grandpa Max to the boys.

"Be careful of what?" she snapped. "What does this mean—that was a close one?"

"Not now," replied Grandpa Max. "Some other time—"

Jeanne pointed an accusing finger at Grandpa Max and Bobby.

"There is something very funny going on here and I want to know—"

"Not now!" exclaimed Grandpa Max.

Jeanne knitted her eyebrows, crossed her arms and plopped onto the nearest chair.

"If you do not tell me…then I refuse to guide D'Artagnan to the docks of Calais!"

Chapter Eleven
The Cardinal

Porthos' face reddened while attempting to squeeze his ample frame into a chair near the fireplace.

"How is it that the second most powerful man in France can't afford bigger chairs?" he cried.

"Be quiet and drink your wine," replied Aramis, who seemed irritated that his large friend had interrupted his conversation with Athos.

"I think I am stuck in this accursed chair!" Porthos jumped to his feet with the chair wedged firmly around his backside. Athos and Aramis laughed out loud upon seeing their friend's dilemma.

Porthos narrowed his eyes at his companions before pushing the chair's narrow arms with all of his might. The chair wouldn't budge. "If you two could stop laughing for one moment, I could use a little help!"

"Hold still," said the still laughing Aramis.

"Turn around, Porthos!" exclaimed Athos.

Before Aramis and Athos could maneuver Porthos into a better position to extricate his ample lower torso from the clinging chair, the door flew open. Two of the Cardinal's guards marched deliberately through the doorway only to stop abruptly at the sight of poor Porthos and his two friends wrestling with the chair.

"What is this?" inquired one of the smirking guards. He was a tall man with a narrow face and thin mustache. The guard raised his hand to conceal his laughter.

Porthos bristled. "Don't just stand there looking like a fool," he shouted at the guard. "Help us!"

The second guard didn't even try to conceal his laughter.

"You dare laugh at a King's Musketeer!" cried Athos. "I demand satisfaction!"

The first guard's face quickly reddened. "Please forgive me, Monsieur Athos, but you will have to admit that this does appear…"

Aramis finished the guard's comment. "Funny?"

"Get me out of this!" screamed Porthos who was growing more and more frustrated by the second.

"How dare you insult my friend, Porthos!" threatened Athos as he moved away from his friends toward the door. Aramis quickly understood Athos' intent; he grabbed Porthos by the arm and followed Athos' lead.

"If I had my sword," Athos continued, still edging toward the door, "I would dispatch you both!"

The guards spread their arms and bowed politely.

"Please excuse us, dear Athos," said one of the guards. "We meant no disrespect."

Athos calmed. "That is more like it," he said brightly as he returned the guard's bow. "Would you care to join us and share some of our delightful Spanish wine?"

"Athos!" exclaimed Porthos, who continued to struggle with the obstinate chair. "Have you forgotten the task at hand?"

Athos smiled broadly at Porthos. "Ah, how could I forget?" He turned toward the two guards and said, "As much as I would like nothing more than to offer you some wine, it seems that we have a…predicament. Would you be so kind as to help my unfortunate friend free himself from his unlikely bonds?"

The guards and Athos laughed heartily.

"Of course," said one of the guards. "We would do most anything for a sip of Spanish wine."

Athos and the guards laughed again.

"Come then!" cried the musketeer. "Free poor Porthos and we shall drink until dawn."

"Aye!" exclaimed the guards.

Athos led the guards behind Porthos. "If you would please each grab one of the chair's legs," he said cheerfully.

The guards obeyed without question. Each grasped one leg of Porthos' chair tightly and made ready to pull.

"Good," continued Athos. "My comrade and I will take a firm grip of poor Porthos' arms." Athos waved his hand merrily in the air. "On three gentlemen, we shall pull in the opposite direction. Ready?" The guards nodded. Athos turned to Aramis and Porthos and winked. His companions smiled.

"One!" he called out loudly. "Two!" Athos nearly sang the word. "THREE!"

Athos and Aramis held fast to their companion's thick arms as the two guards strained against the firmly fixed chair.

"Pull!" cried Aramis.

"Harder!" yelled Athos.

The guards pulled harder and harder. The chair was beginning to move and in another instant, Porthos could feel it pull free from his aching posterior. The guards, with the chair still in hand, fell backward in a heap onto the floor. The guards laughed heartily as they tossed the chair away.

"Porthos!" cried Athos.

The large musketeer leapt over the chair and landed on the two unsuspecting guards.

The taller, mustached guard started to scream. "What—?"

In a flash, Porthos had grabbed the guards by the collar and smashed their heads together, knocking them out—cold.

"Aramis!" said Athos. "Their swords—quickly!"

Aramis ripped the blades from their sheaths and tossed one to Athos.

"What about me?" groused Porthos.

Athos laughed and pointed toward the table.

"You bring the wine, my large friend," Athos said brightly. "Come, let us find D'Artagnan!"

The three companions bolted through the unguarded doorway. The dimly lit hallway was deserted, without a guard in sight. From the entrance to their temporary prison, the hallways ran in three different directions: the right, the left and straight ahead. Since the musketeers had been brought there blindfolded, they could not be sure of which route would lead them to safety.

"This way!" commanded Porthos pointing down the hallway straight ahead.

"No, no," cried Aramis, "to the right!"

"The left!" countered Athos.

"No, this way," growled Porthos, his arm still pointing down the hallway directly ahead.

"No, this way!" exclaimed Athos.

"Athos," snapped Aramis.

"What?"

"I think Porthos is correct."

"Why?" inquired Athos incredulously.

"Look!" exclaimed Aramis, as he extended his arms to point down the left and right hallways.

With swords drawn, three guards rushed headlong through each hallway, quickly bearing down on the musketeers. Athos slapped Porthos on the shoulder and said, "For once, my large friend, I am inclined to agree with you. Come!"

In an instant, the three musketeers had bolted down the hallway ahead. Six of the Cardinal's guards crowded into the narrow hallway in hot pursuit.

"Arrest them!" cried one of the guards.

Aramis glanced over his shoulder. "Hurry, they gain on us!"

Athos led the way, his eyes darting from side to side in search of an escape route.

"What shall we do?" grunted Porthos, who still clutched the two bottles of Spanish wine.

"This way!" shouted Athos as he darted down another deserted hallway.

"We need to slow them down somehow," panted Aramis.

Athos glanced at Aramis and smiled. "That's it!" he cried. "Porthos! Drop the wine!"

"What?" snapped Porthos. "The wine?"

"Quickly, drop the bottles."

"But, the wine—"

"DROP THEM, PORTHOS!" shouted Aramis.

"Throw them down the hall," snapped Athos.

Porthos reluctantly obeyed his friends, and let the bottles fly down the narrow hallway. As the unsuspecting pursuers followed them around the corner, the guard in the lead stepped on one of the bottles causing him to trip and fall backwards onto his companions. The guards fell into a heap of flailing arms, legs and cries of pain. The musketeers stopped to admire their work.

"Ha!" exclaimed Athos. "It worked."

"Well done, good Porthos," said Aramis.

Porthos scratched his head thoughtfully. "But the wine—"

"If we get out of this mess, my large friend," said the smiling Athos, "I will happily buy you your fill."

Porthos nodded sadly. "Now what?"

"Let us get around the next corner before our friends back there recover enough to resume the chase."

The three friends veered around into the adjoining hallway. This hall was far brighter than the ones they had just been chased through. Athos pointed toward a large, ornate door.

"Quickly," he whispered as he lunged for the shiny brass knob. "We'll hide in here!"

Athos pushed open the door, allowing Aramis and Porthos to file into the room after him. Porthos closed the door gently behind them. The comrades stood with their ears close to the smooth wood listening intently for any sound of the guards.

"May I help you?" asked a smooth voice, startling the intruders.

"Huh?" grunted Porthos.

Athos and Aramis turned and placed their backs to the door. A lone figure sat at a large, oaken desk placed in the room's farthest corner. The quarters were so dimly lit that the musketeers hadn't noticed him. The man rose from his chair and stepped out from behind the desk. He was *not* a guard. With his red robes and jeweled cross that hung stiffly from his neck, he could only be of the church.

"Ah," said the man sarcastically. "If I am not mistaken, you are Athos, Porthos and Aramis, the most famous of His Majesty's Musketeers. I see you have escaped my guards."

"Cardinal Richelieu!" exclaimed Athos.

Chapter Twelve
The Road from Paris

Jeanne's eyes narrowed at Bobby and Grandpa Max.

"I'm serious," she threatened through clenched teeth. "If you don't tell me, I refuse to go!"

Bobby spread his arms out wide. "Aw c'mon, Jeanne."

"But, D'Artagnan needs your help," added Grandpa Max.

Jeanne turned her head pretending not to hear. Bobby stepped closer.

"You need D'Artagnan…" Bobby paused, "and the Three Musketeers to free your father."

Jeanne folded her arms across her chest even tighter. A tear formed in the one eye that Bobby could see. Grandpa Max noticed.

"Without D'Artagnan," Max said softly, "you may never see your father again."

Tears streamed down the girl's rosy cheeks.

"I just want to know what is happening here," snapped Jeanne. "You people speak and act so funny…" Her voice trailed off beneath the weight of the tears.

Grandpa Max placed his hand upon her shoulder. "Let me just say that we are from very, very far away."

Bobby gazed into Jeanne's eyes. "You've got to trust us, Jeanne," he said softly. "D'Artagnan needs your help. *We* need your help."

Jeanne returned Bobby's gaze for a moment before forcing both ends of her full lips into a smile. She nodded, still trying to sniff away her tears.

"Oh brother!" snarled Fritzy. "Bobby's gone and got all mushy on us."

"Isn't he the ladies man!" laughed Keith.

Bobby swung around to face his friends. "Shut up, you guys!" cried the flush-faced Bobby.

"Now, now boys…" said Grandpa Max while trying to keep from laughing himself.

Jeanne's reddened cheeks brightened around her smile. She even started to laugh.

Bobby turned back. "So, you're okay?"

Jeanne nodded again.

Just then, D'Artagnan burst into the room.

"Planchet has arranged for our transportation from Paris," he said brightly. "Come! We must be going."

Everyone followed D'Artagnan through the apartment's narrow doorway. The afternoon sun filled the rustic avenue with the long shadows of the apartments above. People bustled along the walkways, but not one took the least bit of interest in the tiny group. Bobby glanced up and down the street. No one even looked their way—it was as if they were invisible.

"So where's our transportation?" inquired Bobby, remembering that in the book the King's Musketeers always had the finest steeds to ride. "All I see is a rickety old wagon and two old swaybacked horses."

"Oui," replied D'Artagnan, "this *is* our means of transport."

"That old thing!" cried Fritzy.

D'Artagnan nodded with a smile as he gestured toward the broken down wagon. Small and painted a grayish-black, it looked horribly worse for the wear. A gray, rotted staircase led down from a small door to the rear.

Jeanne was aghast. "This wagon will never get us to the coast," she said impatiently.

"Shhh," hissed D'Artagnan. "This is just to get us out of Paris."

"Then what?" asked Bobby.

D'Artagnan hopped up onto one of the gray steps, making it creak loudly. He leaned over and whispered, "I have arranged to have my lackey, Planchet, meet us with some fine horses to take us on our journey."

"Why the wagon?" asked Bobby. "Why not just ride the horses?"

"The Cardinal's men will be searching the city for us," replied the Gascon. "Especially the one with the big nose we left tied up in the alley. He has always hated my companions and I." D'Artagnan opened the door and gestured for everyone to enter. "Max, there are disguises for you and Jeanne inside. Can you drive one of these?"

"I suppose so, why?" replied Bobby's grandfather.

"I want you and Jeanne up in front. The boys and I will ride in the back." D'Artagnan paused. "Remember Max, if we are stopped Jeanne is your granddaughter, I am your son and the boys…Jeanne's cousins."

"Would it not be smarter to leave under the cover of night?" asked Max.

D'Artagnan rubbed his chin and replied, "I had thought of that, but I believe that is what Richelieu will be expecting."

"Aye," said Max. "I understand."

"I hope this works," said Bobby.

"Don't worry," said the Frenchman. "It will."

"What of my father?" inquired Jeanne, as another tiny tear formed in the corner of her eye. The tear ran slowly down her cheek and D'Artagnan leaned in and gallantly brushed it away with his thumb.

"Do not worry, my little one," he said softly. "My companions and I will not let any harm come to your father."

Jeanne's face flushed crimson. "I am not so little," she snapped.

Fritzy elbowed Bobby in the ribs.

"Ow," he grunted. "What was that for?"

"Oh nothin'," replied Fritzy slyly.

"Oh, I get it," whispered Bobby. "You think that Jeanne's got the hots for D'Artagnan."

Keith quickly added his two cents. "You know what my dad always says, 'if the shoe fits, wear it'."

Bobby shoved Keith. "You're full of it, and so is your dad!"

Fritzy whispered something in Keith's ear. Both boys started to laugh.

Jeanne glanced languidly over her shoulder and sighed, *"Boys."*

The trip through the bustling streets of Paris was slow. A day full of carriage traffic and an unsure driver made the short journey seem like days instead of hours. D'Artagnan sat, concealed by a ratty red curtain, just behind Grandpa Max. Peering through a small hole he had Planchet cut in the curtain, D'Artagnan was able to see well enough to guide Max along the busy Paris streets.

On Grandpa Max's orders, Bobby, Fritzy and Keith kept watch along the walkways through the wagon's warped, wooden slats. It didn't really serve any purpose, but it was the only thing that Bobby's grandfather could think of to keep the boys occupied and quiet.

"How much further?" Grandpa Max asked D'Artagnan without turning around.

D'Artagnan maneuvered the curtain so he could see the shops along the street. "I cannot see very well. Is that a church on the corner to the right?" he inquired.

"Yes," replied Max.

"Then I think we will be to the city's limit within the hour."

Jeanne turned toward the curtain. "I think we should go a different way," she said urgently. "Where must we meet Planchet?"

D'Artagnan's head poked through a split in the curtain.

"This avenue will take us to the edge of Paris," he said. "Planchet waits for us in a grove of trees just beyond the river."

"But, I believe this way to be dangerous," said Jeanne softly. "My father had said—"

D'Artagnan shook his head.

"No," he growled. "We stay on this road. It is the fastest way." He turned to Jeanne and smiled. "Paris I know; it is the path to the channel that I do not."

Jeanne's eyes twinkled at the sight of D'Artagnan's winning smile. Her voice nearly sang. "Whatever you wish, D'Artagnan."

"I told you she liked D'Artagnan," whispered Fritzy as he dug his elbow sharply into Bobby's ribs.

"Ow!" cried Bobby.

"*Whatever you wish,*" Fritzy chided. "Yeah sure, Bobby. She doesn't have the hots for D'Artagnan."

"Shut up, Fritzy!" said Bobby while rubbing his bruised ribs.

"Come in, come in," said Cardinal Richelieu. "I am sure it will only be a moment before my guards arrive." Richelieu pushed away from his desk and rose to his feet; the flickering flame of the desk lamp cast eerie shadows against the man's sunken cheeks.

"Your Eminence!" exclaimed Aramis. "We had no idea—"

"Of course, how could you?" answered the Cardinal. Richelieu walked around his desk into the light of the room.

The middle aged man smiled broadly causing the ends of his curled mustache to reach his eyes. He stroked his pointed goatee. "Would you care for some wine?"

Porthos stepped forward. "That sounds goo—"

"We have had enough wine!" exclaimed Athos. "We would like our freedom!"

Richelieu nodded thoughtfully. "I understand," he said with an open gesture of his hands, "but, I am afraid that will be impossible."

Athos raised his sword, gently pressing the tip against Richelieu's chest.

"Athos, no!" cried Aramis. "You cannot harm—"

"Quiet, Aramis!" shouted Athos.

"It is too late," said the Cardinal. "Your friend, D'Artagnan, has already left the city—"

"He goes alone?" growled Porthos.

Richelieu politely covered his mouth and chuckled.

"Not exactly," he replied. "It seems that your friend has met up with three new companions to help him reach Buckingham—"

"Never!" Porthos growled again.

"Oh, but he has." Richelieu placed one finger gingerly upon Athos' blade and pushed it away. He moved toward the fireplace and rubbed his hands briskly as if he were warming them. "It seems that he has taken up with three young boys who claim to be King's Musketeers."

The three companions shot each other a questioning glance.

Athos shook his head. "Do not take me lightly, Your

Eminence—"

"I am quite serious!" The Cardinal turned away from the fire as if satisfied that his hands had been properly warmed. A grin split his mustached face. Richelieu's eyes twinkled in the soft light. "Three boys, an old man and a young girl, I believe."

"This is nonsense!" huffed Porthos.

Aramis stepped forward. "I think not," he said thoughtfully. "I think he is being truthful—"

Suddenly, a great racket filled the hallway outside the door.

"The guards!" exclaimed Porthos. Athos' eyes darted around the room in search of escape.

Richelieu laughed. "There is no way out but through that door." The noise and clatter increased in the hallway.

"Not likely," said Aramis brightly. "Powerful men like you always possess secret passageways."

Athos spotted the long curtains behind Richelieu's desk.

"Aramis, Porthos," he barked, "behind the curtains— quickly!" Without so much as a word, his companions maneuvered around the desk and threw open the crimson draperies. Aramis waved the tip of his sword in the direction of Cardinal Richelieu's chair and said, "If Your Eminence would be so kind as to take his seat."

Richelieu shook his head and shrugged. "As you wish," he said, "but you *will* not escape."

"We *will* see," replied Athos as Cardinal Richelieu arranged his brightly colored robes and returned to his chair. "I will be right behind you with my blade resting just between your shoulder blades. Please do not cause me to do anything that I might regret."

Athos joined Aramis and Porthos behind the curtain. The Musketeer, being true to his word, placed the blade exactly where he had promised. Richelieu winced as the point pierced his thick robe and pressed against his skin.

Within seconds, the room filled with the sound of a firm rap on the door.

"Your Eminence," said a muffled voice.

"Come!" growled Richelieu.

The door burst open. It was a small man. His sword was drawn and his manner was urgent.

"Th-the prisoners have g-gotten away, Your Eminence." The guard's voice stammered, and trembled from fright. That was understandable considering that Cardinal Richelieu was the second most powerful man in all of France.

The Cardinal raised his hand. "I kno—" he began before feeling Athos' blade press boldly against his back— Richelieu coughed. "I mean—I want them caught and placed under guard—immediately."

"At once, Your Eminence," saluted the guard.

"Now go!" added the Cardinal impatiently.

The guard swung around and stepped into the hallway.

Athos pressed the blade harder. "Wait!" shouted Richelieu. The guard spun like a top and stepped back into the room.

"Yes, Your Eminence?"

Richelieu twitched as he felt Athos' blade dig deeper into his skin, Athos whispered something to His Eminence.

"What is that you have tucked under your arm?" inquired the Cardinal innocently.

The guard held out a dark bottle. "Spanish wine, Your Eminence. The prisoners used it to make their escape—"

"Never mind—" The Cardinal felt the blade press harder. "Leave the bottle!"

"Yes, Your Eminence." The guard tip-toed toward Cardinal Richelieu and said, "I'll leave it on your desk."

"Excellent—now go!"

The guard bowed three times before reaching the door. In another second, he was gone.

Athos stepped out from behind the drapery and sat confidently on the edge of the desk.

"Why you impertinent fool!" scolded Richelieu.

Athos laughed heartily. "I have been called much worse than that, Your Eminence," he said smugly.

Porthos reached around the Cardinal and snatched the bottle of wine.

"Ah," he sighed. "Now we have something to keep us warm on the road from Paris."

"You will never escape my palace alive," Richelieu said sharply.

"I think we will, Your Eminence," said Athos pointing toward Porthos. "You see, my comrade here found a secret panel behind the drapes." Athos rubbed his chin. "If my memory serves me correctly, I believe the rumor is that your secret passage leads to the stables." He yanked off the crimson ribbon that adorned the curtain. "Aramis, would you be so kind as to bind His Eminence to his chair."

As Aramis busied himself with the task, Porthos gladly gagged Cardinal Richelieu with a lacy handkerchief that he had found on the desk.

"Now, Your Eminence," said Athos, "my comrades and I will be taking our leave, as well as three of your finest mounts to the quickest road away from Paris." Athos turned to his comrades. "All for one!" he cried.

"One for all!" they sang in unison.

Chapter Thirteen
The Road to Calais

Bobby led the way as he and the others climbed from the wagon. He rubbed his sore backside as soon as his numbed feet hit the ground. The last few miles through Paris had been extremely bumpy and Grandpa Max's lack of expertise as a wagon driver became more than evident with every mile.

Fritzy and Keith jumped down from the steps, both giving a loud grunt as their feet met the dusty road. D'Artagnan emerged from the wagon wearing a smile from ear to ear. He obviously thought it was funny that the three young boys were so achy from the trip.

"My butt hurts," growled Fritzy, as he stretched his arms straight over his head.

"Me, too," added Keith. "That ride was the pits."

"Quit complaining," Bobby scolded. "I had the worst seat—"

"Oh yeah?" countered Fritzy. "Mine was worse."

D'Artagnan laughed out loud before landing on the soft road with a thud.

"Do you always argue like this?" the Gascon asked brightly.

Keith shot D'Artagnan a crooked smile. "Isn't that what friends do?"

Bobby tugged at D'Artagnan's baggy sleeve. "Didn't you tell us back at Xavier's that you and Athos, Porthos and Aramis kinda fight like we do?"

D'Artagnan threw his head back and laughed loudly. His laugh became infectious and before long, all three boys had happily joined in. Grandpa Max and Jeanne had just appeared at the wagon door as the laughing reached a deafening crescendo.

"*Now* what in the world is going on?" inquired Grandpa Max.

"Nothin', Grandpa Max," replied Bobby. "D'Artagnan just made us laugh, that's all—"

"Look!" exclaimed Fritzy. He pointed down the road with great excitement.

All eyes turned.

"Ah," said D'Artagnan as if he were quite satisfied. "It seems Planchet has arrived with our mounts." D'Artagnan turned to gaze at the quickly setting sun. "And right on time, I might add."

Bobby and the others watched as D'Artagnan's lackey sped toward them riding a large, black steed, followed closely by five magnificent horses. One was gray, two were chestnut, and the two others were dark brown. The sound of the horses' hoofs thundered against the soft dirt road, their manes flowing wildly in the wind. Bobby turned to his grandfather and smiled. Grandpa Max nodded. The adventure just kept getting better.

"This is so cool!" exclaimed Fritzy.

Smoky dust filled the air above the road. Bobby and Keith rubbed the dirt from their eyes. Planchet brought the horses to a sliding halt, throwing up even more muck. Grandpa Max and the kids began to choke on the churning, swirling dust. D'Artagnan rushed to assist Planchet with the mounts.

"Quickly," said the Gascon over his shoulder. "We must hurry."

Keith tripped over his feet while backing away from the horses; his face appeared pasty. "I-I-I've never ridden a horse before," he said fearfully.

Fritzy patted the nose of the black beauty that Planchet was riding.

"Sure you have." Fritzy was grinning from ear to ear. "Don't you remember the pony rides at the carnival?"

"That was a long time ago," snapped Keith.

"I thought it was just last summer," joked Bobby.

Keith's face turned purple. He looked as if he were about to burst. "*Ha, ha!*" he shouted loudly. "*Very funny!*"

Bobby and Fritzy shot each other a quick glance.

"*We* thought so!" they said in unison, before laughing loudly.

Bobby turned to his grandfather. "This is the greatest time I've ever had, Grandpa Max." He spoke softly so the others wouldn't hear. "Will it work with all of your books?"

Max shook his head. "Only the ones that I purchased from the old woman...I think." Grandpa Max's expression turned serious as he searched his grandson's beaming eyes. "Remember," he said, with a tone of caution in his hushed voice. Max placed his hand on the boy's shoulder and led him away from the others. "Even though we are inside a novel, the things that happen here are real—*very real!*"

"What do you mean?" asked Bobby as he turned his head to watch Fritzy and Jeanne push poor Keith closer to his waiting, large, chestnut colored mount. The horse whinnied and shook his head from side to side. Keith jumped nearly a foot in the air.

Bobby chuckled until he felt a sharp pain sting the back of his arm. "Ouch!" he cried.

"You see, Bobby..." said Grandpa Max, as he pulled his hand away from his grandson's burning arm.

Bobby rubbed his skin furiously. "Why did you pinch me?"

"...You can feel."

"So?"

Grandpa Max shook his head. "If you could feel the pinch of my finger..." His voice trailed off. Grandpa Max's tone was tense, sobering. His eyes narrowed. Bobby gasped; he had never seen his grandfather look so serious. "...Then you can feel the point of a sword." Grandpa Max pointed toward Fritzy and Keith. "Make sure your friends understand."

"But, Grandpa Max—"

Max waved his hand anticipating his grandson's protest. "I know, I know," he replied. "I believe this to be fun too, but… I'm not so sure we're doing the right thing."

Bobby wrinkled his nose. "I don't understand—"

"We've changed the book!"

"But I thought that the book had already changed when the Cardinal captured Athos, Porthos and Aramis…" Bobby's voice trailed off thoughtfully. "…That's what you were saying before you disappeared!"

"Exactly, this entire mess is my fault." Grandpa Max drew away from Bobby. His chin settled upon his guilt-filled chest.

Bobby followed close on his grandfather's heels. "But how?"

"It seems," began Grandpa Max, "on the day before D'Artagnan was to reveal his plan to his companions, he asked me, in Planchet's absence, to deliver a note to Monsieur Athos instructing him to gather Aramis and Porthos at an appointed time and place." Max worriedly rubbed the back of his neck and shook his head. "I was spotted by two of the Cardinal's Guards. They must have thought I looked suspicious so they chased me."

"Did they catch you?"

"They didn't have to. In my haste to escape, I dropped the note—"

Bobby gasped. "And they found it!"

Grandpa Max nodded. "So you see, this whole thing is my fault."

Bobby grabbed his grandfather's arm and spun him around.

"Then I guess there's only one thing left to do."

"What *can* we do?" pleaded Grandpa Max.

"Fix it!"

"Come, you two!" called out D'Artagnan. "Let us be on our way."

Bobby and Grandpa Max started back toward the group. Planchet held the reins of two noble looking steeds. Dark brown and muscled, the horses looked well suited for the journey ahead. As Planchet assisted Bobby and his grandfather into each of their saddles, Bobby glanced over at his friends. Fritzy beamed with delight as he sat atop his gray mount. Keith, on the other hand, looked as pale as a ghost. Even his trembling lips appeared a pasty pink as Keith shook in his saddle.

"You okay?" Bobby asked his wobbly friend.

"I-I-I think so," replied the frightened Keith.

"He'll be fine!" declared D'Artagnan. "By the time we reach Calais, this little Musketeer will be an excellent horseman."

Everyone laughed—everyone but Keith, of course.

"The plot thickens, my friends," continued D'Artagnan. "The lackeys of Athos, Porthos and Aramis have been arrested. They, along with Planchet, were to follow us on our journey." The Gascon frowned. "Alas, we are on our own. What say you all?"

No one spoke. Grandpa Max froze in his saddle. Bobby's back stiffened. Silence descended upon the group like a thick blanket of clouds.

Bobby's chest heaved with a great sigh. "I say, all for one!" he cried.

D'Artagnan and the others smiled. At least Keith tried to smile before they all answered, "And one for all!"

With Jeanne and D'Artagnan leading the way, the brave band sped upon thundering hoofs toward Calais.

* * *

"Ouch!" cried Porthos. He had bumped his head upon a hanging beam. The large musketeer rubbed his forehead then examined his hand. "At least there is no blood," he snapped.

"Be quiet!" scolded Aramis, who stood just behind Porthos.

"But my head—"

"Hush, Porthos!" hissed Athos from up ahead.

The secret passage from the Cardinal's rooms proved to be dark and narrow. The soft odor of dampened wood and dirt filled the three companion's nostrils.

"It is too dark, Athos," complained Porthos. "We shall never find our way."

Athos pushed ahead into the darkness. "I can smell horses, I tell you!" It was faint, but the heavy scents of hay and manure began to tickle Athos's nose. "Do you smell it?"

Porthos and Aramis plunged ahead blindly following their companion.

"Yes, I smell it too," said Aramis, "but I thought it was Porthos."

Athos laughed out loud. Porthos only narrowed his eyes.

As they stumbled down the dark passage, the aroma of the stable grew stronger. Before long, the passageway brightened. The blackness and shadows of the secret shaft slowly turned to gray and the grays turned to color. Their hearts brightened as well. Better able to see, they quickened the pace.

"Look there!" cried Athos. "A door! The light is coming through the cracks."

They rushed toward the light.

"The devil!" snapped Athos upon reaching the door first and finding it locked.

"There must be a handle, a switch, something to open it!" cried Porthos.

"Shhh," hissed Aramis as he placed his ear up against the door. "I hear voices."

The Three Musketeers fell silent.

"Two, maybe three guards," whispered Athos.

"It doesn't matter how many. We have to get through this door before the guards discover Richelieu," said Aramis softly.

Porthos turned his back to the fixed doorway. "I have to sneeze," he hissed. "The dust… I… ah-ah-ah…"

Aramis placed his finger beneath Porthos' substantial nose just in time to stop him from sneezing. Porthos leaned up against the door and sighed.

"Thank you," he said.

"Please try and control yourself," whispered Athos.

"I can't help it," replied Porthos. "Uh oh… ah-ah-ah," he shut his eyes tightly as Aramis once again rushed to stop the sneeze.

"Are you okay now?" inquired Aramis.

Porthos rubbed his nose and smiled. "Yes, I believe...
ah-ah-ah-CHOO!"

He sneezed so hard that the force of the sneeze pushed
his large frame hard against the locked door. As the panel gave
way, poor Porthos burst through the doorway tumbling out of
control onto a large pile of straw.

Aramis was right, there were three guards and they
were armed. Athos and Aramis rushed through the opening,
swords in hand. Leaping over Porthos, they engaged the guards
with the sound of crashing blades and hollers. Porthos jumped
to his feet to join the attack before realizing that his only
armament was an uncorked bottle of Spanish wine.

Athos battled one of the guards as Aramis struggled
against two. Blades flashed back and forth in the dimly lit
stable, sending the horses into a fit of whinnies and kicks.
Aramis had dropped to one knee just in front of a stall, but
still fought on. The two guards sensed that they had the best of
Aramis and moved in for the kill. Porthos came around the side
of an empty stall and waved at the guards before darting inside.

"Another one!" screamed one of the guards. "I've got
this one—go!"

The second guard broke away from the fight and chased
Porthos into the stall. Having to only battle one guard, Aramis
renewed the fight with great energy, quickly besting the man
with a wound to the leg. Athos easily disarmed his opponent
with a jab to the guard's shoulder.

The third guard, unaware that his companions had been

beaten, rushed into the empty stall in search of Porthos. Except for a thick rope that hung from above, there was nothing in the stall.

"Yoo-hoo," said a voice from above.

The guard looked up just in time to see the bottle of Spanish wine before it smashed against his head, knocking him out cold. The guard hit the straw covered floor with a thud.

"Nice work, Porthos!" shouted Athos to the large musketeer as he shimmied down the rope.

"Pity, though," said Aramis sadly, "such a waste of good Spanish wine."

"Don't I know it," snapped Porthos.

The three companions joked and laughed as they bound and gagged the guards.

"What do you say we saddle up three of the Cardinal's best mounts and speed away from this place?" suggested Athos.

"Where?" inquired Porthos.

"To find D'Artagnan," replied Aramis.

"Yes," began Athos, "if D'Artagnan is to go to London then the docks of Calais is our destination."

Once the horses were saddled and ready, Athos added, "We must each take a different road. I will take the road from Paris to the west. Aramis, you take the road to the north. Porthos, you head for the town of Arras and look for them there. If by tomorrow Aramis and I do not find him, we will look for you on the road from Arras to Calais."

"But there is so much distance to cover," said Aramis. "Can we possibly find him?"

Athos clenched his jaw. "We must!"

Then, for the second time that day, hoofs thundered away from Paris and headed for Calais.

Chapter Fourteen
A Stop to Rest

The group galloped on, pressing ever closer to Calais. The sun was setting quickly and soon there would be only bright stars to light the road, but D'Artagnan pushed Bobby, Grandpa Max and the others on. Bobby felt the wind whistle through his hair as he urged his mount forward. He pulled his horse up to the front where D'Artagnan and Jeanne led the way. His stirrups were nearly touching Jeanne's as their horses sped down the path.

"It's getting dark!" he cried out, hoping to be heard over thundering hoofs. "Shouldn't we stop soon?"

Jeanne glanced at Bobby before turning toward D'Artagnan who appeared not to hear. She called out, voicing Bobby's concerns. The Gascon nodded.

Jeanne turned back to Bobby. "There is an inn up

ahead," she shouted over the sound of the galloping hoofs. "We will stay there for the night."

Within moments the sun was gone. Bright orange glowed low across the graying western sky; the day had taken its last gasp. Soon the road would be dark and dangerous. Bobby glanced at Jeanne; she didn't seem to be the least bit concerned about the darkness slowly closing in around them.

In another moment Bobby knew why. There were lights directly ahead. *The inn! Jeanne really does know where she's going.* He glanced at Jeanne once again and saw that she was already looking at him. A sly grin appeared on Jeanne's freckled face. Her eyes sparkled. Bobby was grateful for the waning light because his face had flushed at the very sight of her smile.

The group pulled up the horses in front of the small inn. The compound consisted of three buildings: an inn built from logs and thatch, a barn and a small storage shack. As D'Artagnan dismounted, a small round man rushed onto the front porch, briskly rubbing his hands together.

"Welcome, welcome!" he exclaimed. The man must have been the innkeeper because he began to bark orders loudly.

"Antoine!" cried the round little man. "Six horses if you please?"

Before Grandpa Max and the kids could dismount, a tall figure with stringy, shoulder length hair burst through the barn doors and ran toward them while still pulling up his pants. The tall man helped Jeanne from her saddle as Bobby and the others jumped to the ground.

"Thank you, Antoine," purred the innkeeper as he watched his man lead the horses toward the barn. "I believe we woke up poor Antoine." The innkeeper giggled. "Please come in, come in," he said brightly. "Is it rooms and refreshments you need?"

Bobby was first inside the tiny inn. The main room, though dimly lit, was well appointed and clean. A large stone fireplace on the far wall housed a crackling fire that took the chill out of the evening air. Pleasant scents of cooking game birds and pastries tickled his nostrils. Bobby couldn't remember the last time they had all eaten. It must have been this morning, but so much had happened that day that it was difficult to say. Long, rolling growls rumbled in his stomach so loudly that he was sure the others could hear them.

The small round figure of the innkeeper waddled by Bobby so quickly, that he seemed a blur.

"Francois!" yelled the small round man, motioning toward a large oaken table. "Six for sup."

The evening passed quietly around the large oak table. Keith was still trying to recover from hours of bouncing in the saddle. Fritzy was so hungry, he couldn't shove the food into his mouth fast enough. Grandpa Max asked him more than once where he could possibly be putting it. Bobby sat quietly; he had forgotten his hunger while watching the animated Jeanne flirt with D'Artagnan.

"What's the matter?" Fritzy asked Bobby between bites. "Aren't you hungry?"

Bobby's eyes narrowed. "Nope!"

"Man," continued Fritzy eagerly, "I'm starving…" he

paused as he suddenly became aware of what was bothering his friend. "You're really hooked, aren't you?"

Bobby shook his head. "What are you talkin' about?"

Fritzy smiled. "You know exactly what I'm *talkin'* about—Jeanne!"

"Shut up and eat, Fritzy!" snapped Bobby.

Fritzy smiled again.

Bobby felt a tug on his arm—it was Keith. He pointed his thumb over his shoulder in the direction of the front door.

"Check these guys out," whispered Keith.

Bobby snuck a quick look over his shoulder—just enough to see three dark looking characters standing in the front hallway. Each was dressed in black leather and were well equipped with sword and pistol. The darkness and distance made it difficult to see the men's faces. Then, when one of the men turned toward the fire to greet the innkeeper, his features glowed against the flames. Bobby's back stiffened.

The innkeeper showed the three strangers to a table at the opposite side of the room. Bobby could not help but notice their repeated glances in his direction. He quickly caught D'Artagnan's attention, whose eyebrow was already raised. There was no doubt D'Artagnan recognized the man as well. It was the tall guard with the large nose that led the attack on them in the alley on the way to the Gascon's room. The man's nose was still bruised and swollen from the blow delivered by the bin-cover wielding Grandpa Max.

D'Artagnan, acting as if nothing was wrong, smiled nonchalantly as he whispered to the group.

"Do not act alarmed, my friends," he began, "but danger

is afoot. The Cardinal's guards have arrived."

Keith and Grandpa Max moved to look around the room. Fritzy dropped his fork.

"No, no, my friends," cautioned D'Artagnan, his thin lips still turned up, smiling brightly as he spoke. "We do not want them to know that we are aware of their presence. You must act as if you are enjoying yourselves."

As the evening progressed, the large nosed guard and his lackeys never budged. One, or all, shot menacing glances at D'Artagnan, the three boys and particularly Grandpa Max.

Finally, after the meal was finished, D'Artagnan stood.

"I think it is time for us to get some rest," he said calmly.

Bobby began to protest. "But what about—"

"Do not argue with me, young man!" D'Artagnan spoke loudly as if he were scolding Bobby. The boy understood immediately—the Gascon *wanted* to be heard. They were supposed to be a family and D'Artagnan was playing his part. "It is time we all went to bed," he continued, still speaking loudly.

The innkeeper waddled ahead while leading the way from the dining area to the sleeping rooms. Bobby took one more glance over his shoulder. The large guard's gaze was firmly fixed on the group's every move.

Jeanne had her own room while D'Artagnan, Grandpa Max and the boys slept in an adjoining apartment. After such an exhausting day, even the specter of the tall, bulbous nosed guard and his companions staying at the same inn could not keep them from their much needed sleep—all except for three.

Bobby lay in the warmth of the hay-filled mattress

tossing and turning to the rattling sounds of D'Artagnan's and Grandpa Max's loud snores. Especially Grandpa Max's! His snores finished with a less than delicate whistle that pierced his ears and stiffened his back. Sleep seemed all but impossible.

Then, Bobby heard the faint whisper of his name being called. He popped up, his chest pounding like a drum. He could actually hear his heart thump over the horrible snoring.

"Fritzy, is that you?" he replied in a whisper.

"Shhhh," hissed the voice. "Of course it's me, you big dope!"

Careful not to make a sound, Bobby pushed his blanket aside and slipped out of bed. A sharp shiver ran up his spine as his warm, bare feet met the icy cold floor.

Quietly, so as not to disturb D'Artagnan and Grandpa Max, he tiptoed over to Fritzy's bed. Keith was already perched atop the crude, wooden footboard.

"What are you guys doin' up?" asked Bobby.

"Shhhh," Fritzy hissed again.

"Sorry," Bobby replied in a hushed tone. "What's going on?" Bobby's eyes had become accustomed to the room's inky darkness, bringing his friends into view.

Fritzy grabbed Bobby's shoulder. "We need a plan."

"A what?"

"We need a plan to help D'Artagnan get away from the Cardinal's guards."

"I know," whispered Bobby, "the one with the big nose looked pretty angry."

Keith covered his mouth to keep from giggling out loud. "Wouldn't you be," he said once he got his chuckling under control, "after what Grandpa Max did to his nose?"

Bobby was about to speak, but hesitated a moment.

"Look, guys," he said finally, "we're not the real Three Musketeers, we're just kids. I think we'd better just listen to D'Artagnan—"

"What about the 'all for one and one for all' jazz?" growled Fritzy.

"Yeah!" added Keith.

"Fritzy," snarled Bobby through clenched teeth. "You are not really Porthos—"

"I can at least try to be!"

"What can we do?" inquired Keith.

Fritzy smiled in the darkness—more of a smirk filled with mischief and trouble. Bobby had seen that look before and it left an empty feeling in his gut.

"I think I have an idea," whispered Fritzy. "Bobby, you and Keith…"

Breakfast the next morning included more of the same. The Cardinal's guards sat patiently waiting for the right moment to pounce. Bobby glanced at Fritzy. Fritzy raised an eyebrow at Keith. Grandpa Max knew immediately that the boys were acting strangely. Max leaned in toward the center of the table.

"You boys are up to something," growled Bobby's grandfather. "I just know it!"

Bobby answered first. "Us?" he said while innocently glancing back and forth at his two friends.

Grandpa Max narrowed his eyes. "Oh, I know it," he

said sternly. "Promise that you won't do anything foolish—"

"Uh, oh," said D'Artagnan. The large guard with the bulbous nose was up and moving menacingly toward their table. "Everyone is to be on their guard."

"Excuse me," said the guard politely. "You all look so familiar…is it possible that I may know you from somewhere?"

Grandpa Max rose slowly from his chair. "I am sure that Monsieur is mistaken. We are but a small family of farmers on our way to Calais to start a new life. We could never expect to have the privilege of meeting someone as worldly as you…until now of course."

The guard narrowed his eyes and carefully studied Grandpa Max's face.

"I see," said the guard. "But…you do seem familiar. What is your name?"

"Max, Monsieur," he replied. "And yours?"

The guard snorted in indignation. "That is not important…or your business."

D'Artagnan started to stand.

"Please remain seated, Monsieur," warned the guard, his right hand resting on the grip of his blade. D'Artagnan settled back into his chair. "That is better," continued the guard.

Sweat rolled down Bobby's back. He could smell trouble in the air and he didn't like it. The man knew exactly who they were. The guard was toying with them, as a cat does to a mouse before he gobbles him up. Bobby had to do something… and quickly.

"May we go outside?" he blurted.

The guard took a step back and grinned. Dark, ugly

ridges formed at the corners of his mouth.

"Why, of course," he growled. "Why don't we all step outside? I would love to discuss a little matter that happened in an alleyway in Paris yesterday."

Grandpa Max protested. "But, Monsieur—"

"Outside!" exclaimed the guard.

Bobby shot a quick glance at Fritzy and Keith before bolting for the door. Fritzy and Keith were close on his heels. The guard turned to his companions and pointed toward the boys who had already disappeared through the doorway.

"Boys!" cried Grandpa Max angrily.

"Get them!" cried the guard as he quickly drew his sword and pressed the tip roughly against D'Artagnan's chest. A crimson circle spread slowly around the point. "Please place your sword on the table, Monsieur D'Artagnan!"

The Gascon reluctantly obeyed.

Meanwhile, the two guards followed their orders without question, dashing through the room and knocking over tables, chairs and anything else that may have gotten in their way.

Grandpa Max screamed, desperately hoping to stop his grandson and his friends from doing anything that could bring them harm. "BOBBY!"

The tall guard brought the back of his hand across the old man's face. Grandpa Max stumbled backward. D'Artagnan tried to move but he quickly stopped as he felt the blade penetrate deeper into his skin.

There was a loud crash. The tall guard swung his head around to see what had happened, only to spy his comrades sprawled out on the small porch at the front of the inn. They were being pummeled and kicked by the three boys who had tripped them.

It was at this instant that D'Artagnan decided to strike. In a flash, the Gascon had pulled away from the guard's blade and pushed it and its holder's arm to the side. Before the guard could recover, D'Artagnan had pounced on his sword and was prepared to fight.

Aware that the two swords would start to fly at any second, and that the boys could probably use some help, Max grabbed Jeanne's hand and pulled her toward the door. When they had arrived at the porch, the boys were running toward the barn as the two guards struggled to their feet.

Max pushed Jeanne up against the wall just beside the door. She looked frightened and pale—she trembled as she watched D'Artagnan and the large guard parry and thrust amongst the inn's scattered tables and chairs.

"Stay here!" exclaimed Grandpa Max.

"What of D'Artagnan?" she cried.

Grandpa Max glanced over his shoulder. Then, turning back to the girl, his thin lips turned into smile.

"Don't worry about him. Just stay here!"

Jeanne nodded. Max could see her body shake with fear. He smiled again before exploding through the doorway, stopping suddenly as he reached the porch. The boys were in trouble. Swords drawn, the two guards had them backed up against the barn door. Grandpa Max jumped back into the inn.

"D'Artagnan!" he cried. "They have the boys!"

The Gascon picked up a chair and flung it through the

air. The large guard barely ducked in time, but that one brief moment was long enough for the point of D'Artagnan's blade to find its mark. The guard fell bleeding to the floor.

D'Artagnan studied the guard's wounded leg. "You shall live to fight another day, my friend," he growled. "But if I am not mistaken, Max had asked what your name was."

The guard remained silent. This time it was D'Artagnan who pressed a sharp blade against his opponent's chest.

"Baptiste," gasped the guard as he struggled to catch his breath.

D'Artagnan pointed his sword toward the ceiling, then, lowering it with a flourish said, "Until we meet again, Monsieur Baptiste."

"Okay," growled Fritzy as he stared down the guard's shiny blade. "Whose idea was this anyway?"

Bobby and Keith both stared incredulously at their friend.

"YOURS!" they shouted in unison.

"Oh yeah," said the flush-faced Fritzy.

Keith tugged at Bobby's shirt. Someone was approaching. Bobby shook his head and shrugged as he looked beyond the guards. An extremely large, angry man drew closer.

"Be quiet, rascals," snarled one of the guards, "or I will stick you."

"Do the Cardinal's guards now fight with young boys?" boomed the large stranger's powerful voice.

The guard's faces paled before they swung quickly around to face the man.

"Monsieur Porthos!" exclaimed one guard.

"Mon Dieu!" exclaimed the other.

The boys turned to each other and smiled, but neither Bobby nor Keith smiled as broadly as Fritzy.

"On Guard!" shouted Porthos playfully, as he jumped from his horse.

The two guards raised their swords just as D'Artagnan, Max and Jeanne burst through the doorway.

"Porthos!" exclaimed D'Artagnan.

"Ah, D'Artagnan," returned the large musketeer. "Good to see that you are still alive." The clash of two blades against one echoed through the courtyard. Porthos parried off the two swordsmen's attack. "I see you still have the old man with you. Hello, Max."

D'Artagnan laughed with relief upon seeing his old friend in action once again.

"Take the children and go!" growled Porthos between thrusts and parries. "I will take care of this lot."

The two guards fought valiantly but were no match for the skilled Porthos.

D'Artagnan and Max threw open the barn door. As directed, the stable boy had fed, watered and saddled their mounts while they ate breakfast. Grandpa Max helped Jeanne onto her horse then mounted his own.

"Quickly," cried D'Artagnan to the boys. "Mount up."

Bobby and Keith struggled into their saddles but Fritzy had not budged an inch.

"C'mon, Fritzy!" shouted Bobby. "Let's go!"

Fritzy turned to his friends, grinning from ear to ear.

"I'm staying!" he proclaimed loudly.

Bobby protested. "But, Fritzy—"

"I have to." Fritzy glanced at Porthos and the swordplay that ensued. "He's *my* Musketeer!"

"Fritzy!" shouted Grandpa Max.

"I'm staying!"

"Go!" shouted Porthos as his sword whistled sharply over the two guard's heads. "Go! The boy will be safe with me!"

"GO!" screamed Fritzy.

D'Artagnan smiled as Porthos pointed down the road to Calais. Steering his mount's head in that direction, he motioned for Grandpa Max and the kids to follow.

Bobby looked sadly at his friend. "Bye, Fritzy. Good luck."

"Call me Porthos." Fritzy winked at his friends.

"Yeah," added Keith warmly, "take care of yourself."

"Go!" cried Fritzy as he slapped the backside of Bobby's horse.

Bobby could still hear the clashing of swords over the thunder of horses' hoofs as they sped away. He glanced over his shoulder to catch one last glimpse of Fritzy. Bobby smiled as he watched his good friend rush from the barn, pitchfork in hand, ready to do battle with the Cardinal's guards.

As Bobby turned his eyes away from Fritzy and Porthos, and once again onto the road to Calais and their mission, another horseman sped away from the inn, a horseman who was taking another route—a man with a freshly wounded leg.

Chapter Fifteen
This Isn't Right

As the small group sped from the inn, everyone was thinking about Fritzy—especially Bobby. Fritzy and Keith were his best friends. Losing either one of them was unthinkable, but Fritzy was special to Bobby. They were very close—like brothers.

Bobby's dad would constantly tease Fritzy about always being at their house and Fritzy's mom would say the same about Bobby. Thinking about it, Bobby's chest heaved. It felt as if he would have to swallow his heart to put it back where it belonged.

Jeanne pulled up on the reins and maneuvered her horse even with Bobby's. As their eyes met he sensed her smile was to reassure him that his friend would be all right. Bobby smiled back. He fought back a tear.

Why shouldn't he be okay? he thought. *Fritzy was with*

the biggest, strongest and bravest of all the King's Musketeers.
He nodded at Jeanne.

"He'll be okay!" he shouted over the sound of the
horse's hoofs as they beat impatiently against the weather
hardened, dirt road. "I feel sorry for those two guards."

Jeanne laughed.

Bobby pulled up on his reins and dropped back to Keith.
"He's gonna' be okay!" he shouted.

A thin smile spread across Keith's young face. He
nodded but Bobby couldn't help but notice the large tear that
welled up in his friend's eye. He knew the feeling.

Jeanne once again took the lead. The sun had finally
risen enough to cut the morning chill. They had been on
the road for several hours without rest and the horses were
beginning to show signs of fatigue. Soon their mounts would
need to be fed and watered.

Bobby spotted a fork in the road. The main road went
straight on, but the fork was a small grassy path that led to the
right. Jeanne motioned toward the smaller road then sped down
the narrow pathway. D'Artagnan and Grandpa Max followed
with Bobby and Keith bringing up the rear.

It wasn't long before they arrived at another small inn.
Nestled comfortably in a small grove of trees, the public house
was little more than a small area for the horses to rest and
weary travelers to sit and wash away the dusty road with food
and drink.

D'Artagnan's were the first boots to hit the ground. He
quickly motioned for everyone to stay in the saddle. After a
brief but animated discussion with who appeared to be, by

his smudged and dirty clothes, the stable man, D'Artagnan gestured for all to dismount. The man led the horses to a large, leaky water trough where the animals quickly began to drink their fill.

Satisfied, D'Artagnan led everyone up onto the small shady porch, away from the noonday sun. Five small tables lined the thin log railing that surrounded the rustic covered entrance. Bobby, Keith and Jeanne plopped wearily onto chairs at one of the tables while D'Artagnan and Grandpa Max searched for the innkeeper.

The kids sat quietly as they tried to catch their breath from the long hours in the saddle. Keith's face still appeared pale and the skin below his eyes was gray. Bobby looked at his friend with concern.

"You okay?" he asked Keith. "You look a little pale…" Bobby decided to say no more. There was no sense in making Keith feel worse than he already was.

Keith mumbled something Bobby couldn't quite understand. Finally, Keith forced a smile. "I'll be okay in a minute," he replied softly.

Jeanne reached for Keith's hand. "Maybe a drink of water would make you feel better."

Keith's eyes darted to Bobby as Jeanne's soft, pink hand rested on his. "Yeah…maybe…but I sure could go for a Coke."

"What is this…Coke?" asked Jeanne. "Is it something to drink?"

"Yeah," replied Keith. "I love Coke—ouch!" Bobby had kicked Keith's leg under the table.

"Why did you kick me?" he asked Bobby.

"Did I kick you?" replied Bobby. "I'm sorry, I didn't mean to—"

Keith smiled. "Oh I get it," he said thoughtfully. "No Coke."

Jeanne eyed Bobby suspiciously. "Get what?" she inquired.

"Oh, nothing," replied Bobby. "I wonder where D'Artagnan and Grandpa Max are?" Bobby glanced around nervously looking for any sign of Grandpa Max or D'Artagnan.

Suddenly, there came a loud roar of hoofs and squeaking wheels. A large carriage, drawn by six enormous black horses, thundered down the path and into the small clearing, swirling clouds of dirt into the air. Bobby and the others rubbed their eyes and attempted to cough the dust from their already parched throats. As the carriage driver pulled up on the team's reins, the horses cried out in long, shrill whinnies as they slid to a stop.

"Wow, Bobby!" exclaimed Keith. "Look at those beautiful horses!"

Bobby didn't reply. He was more interested in who the passenger of this ornate, shiny carriage might be. Whoever it was must be of great importance, for guards armed with musket and sword rode beside and behind the gilded coach.

A short, stocky man stepped into view. He must have been standing just around the corner of the building. The man was dressed in black just like Baptiste and the other guards. Without so much as a glance in the kids' direction, the dark figure ambled toward the carriage as if he were afraid to approach whoever had just arrived.

"M'lady," he said brightly, though quite unconvincingly. It was obvious that he was unhappy to see her.

"Athos, Porthos and Aramis have escaped!" growled a woman's voice. "You must beware!"

"Do not fear M'lady," said the man as he tugged at the fingers of his black leather glove. "I can handle them." He removed the glove and pressed his fingers against his thin mustache.

"So thought Baptiste!" said the lady.

"Baptiste?"

"Wounded," she replied. "We met him on the road—"

"Where is he?"

"He will be here soon."

Bobby gulped. "It's Lady de Winter!" he whispered harshly.

"What?" cried Keith.

"Shhhh," hissed Jeanne.

"I'm sure of it—"

"What is she doing here?" asked Keith with a quick glance toward the carriage.

Jeanne narrowed her eyes. "Who is Lady de Winter?"

"She's one of the Richelieu's agents," replied Bobby in a whisper. "This isn't …" Bobby paused. D'Artagnan stepped out onto the porch, eyes narrowed, sword in hand.

"You!" D'Artagnan shouted to the man.

The dark figure's glove dropped to the ground as he spied D'Artagnan's drawn sword.

"Ah," he said brightly, as he bent over and swept the

glove from the ground. "The Gascon!" The man pulled on his glove and drew his sword with a flourish. "We meet again."

Near the town of Meung, this man and his lackeys had robbed D'Artagnan of his father's letter of introduction to Monsieur Treville, commander of His Majesty's Musketeers. D'Artagnan's father and Treville were old friends. It was his hope that this letter would help D'Artagnan become a King's Musketeer. D'Artagnan swore revenge.

"Aye," replied D'Artagnan leaping over the porch's railing and landing on the soft ground with a thud. The Gascon stepped carefully toward the coach. "For the last time, I hope."

Bobby looked at Keith. "This isn't right," he said under his breath.

"I-I know," his friend replied.

Jeanne appeared confused. "What isn't right?"

"Lady de Winter and the man from Meung shouldn't be here—"

"On guard, Monsieur!" shouted D'Artagnan. Both men stood, swords drawn, staring each other down. The air was still, the silence deafening.

Unaware of what was unfolding in front of the inn, Grandpa Max shuffled out the door onto the porch. Bobby sprang from his chair, grabbed his arm and pulled him back inside.

"Wha—?"

"Quiet, Grandpa," hissed Bobby. "Look outside."

Grandpa Max stuck his thin face through the doorway and gasped. He pulled back into the room and leaned up against the open door.

"This is all wrong!" he cried.

"Shhhh!" hissed Bobby. Keith and Jeanne rushed through the doorway.

"My goodness," said Grandpa Max as he swiped the beads of forming sweat from his brow with the back of his hand. "What are *they* doing here? Lady de Winter shouldn't be here or the man from…oh dear…it's worse than I thought—"

Grandpa Max was quickly interrupted by the sound of clashing swords. Blades gleamed, reflecting the sun in a shiny ballet of battle. The man from Meung retreated from D'Artagnan's blade, turned to the carriage driver and yelled, "Go! Take M'Lady from this place." There was no doubt that he expected Athos and Aramis to emerge from the inn at any moment. The carriage took off with a start, leaving only a puff of hazy dust behind. But the two mounted guards stood their ground.

"What do we do, Grandpa?" inquired Bobby as he watched the coach drive away.

"F-first," replied Max, who seemed more than a little shaken. "We give D'Artagnan all the help we can."

"Then what?" inquired Keith.

"We try and put this story back the way it belongs."

Jeanne clutched Bobby's arm tightly. The sword fight had intensified and D'Artagnan was winning. The man from Meung had dropped to his knees; he was no match for D'Artagnan's swift and accurate blade. The two horsemen dismounted and quickly drew their swords.

Jeanne narrowed her eyes. "Could somebody please tell me what you people are talking about?"

"Not now, dear," replied Grandpa Max.

"Uh-oh!" exclaimed Bobby. "The guards just dismounted!"

"Oh my!" gasped Grandpa Max. "We have to help D'Artagnan!"

D'Artagnan jumped away from his opponent to size up the situation. It was three against one. The man from Meung struggled to his feet and lightly dusted the smudges from his knees. He grinned broadly at D'Artagnan.

"Drop your sword!" exclaimed the man from Meung loudly. You are outnumbered and have no chance." He glanced at Grandpa Max and the kids. "Think of the children Monsieur."

D'Artagnan stood in silence, still holding his sword straight and ready for battle. No one made a sound. The air was once again still and quiet. Finally, the brave Gascon dropped his sword to the ground. The man from Meung's thin lips spread evenly across his dark face—an evil, plotting smile.

"That is better," growled the man. "Now, step away." He turned to one of his lackeys. "Get his sword."

As the stocky man to his right started for the sword, the crack of a musket shattered the silent air. Without a sound, the poor man slumped, bleeding to the ground. D'Artagnan snatched up his blade.

"Three against one is quite unfair, Monsieur!" a voice called out loudly. "But two against two...those odds are much more to my liking."

Then the sound of hoofs filled the air as a rider approached. Bobby and Keith hugged the railing to see who it could be. It was another musketeer. Was it Athos? Aramis?

Within a second, the musketeer's horse slid to a stop. He drew his sword and dropped to the ground with one swift movement. The man from Meung and his lackey backed away, glancing around for a better defensive position.

"Aramis!" cried D'Artagnan.

The Musketeer bowed gracefully.

Chapter Sixteen
Aramis

Aramis took his place at D'Artagnan's side. The
man from Meung and his lackey stepped cautiously away,
still searching for the advantage. They faced two of the best
swordsmen in all of France— possibly the world. There was no
advantage to be found.

D'Artagnan struck first with a well placed thrust forcing
the man from Meung back against the large wooden trough.
He did this with such force that water spilled over the edge,
splashing onto the dry ground. In an instant, the lackey moved
against Aramis, who laughed with delight as his sword clashed
loudly against his foe. The lackey was not laughing.

"Grandpa!" cried Bobby, who was glued to the rail to
better see the fight. "We have to do something!"

Grandpa Max rubbed at his forehead nervously while
pacing back and forth along the narrow porch. Bobby couldn't

understand his mumbled reply.

"Wow," gasped Keith, his eyes as wide as saucers. "Is that really Aramis?"

Grandpa Max stopped pacing and glanced absently at the swordsman. "Oh yes," he replied. "That is definitely Aramis."

"Wow," said Keith again. "He's fantastic!"

Bobby turned away from the fight. "Grandpa!" he exclaimed. "What are we going to do?"

The lackey had grown pale with fright. Aramis pursued him with incredible thrusts, pushing him further and further from the porch. The less experienced swordsman tried desperately to parry Aramis' attacks, but the Musketeer was more than even a superior swordsman could handle. It wasn't long before the lackey lay unarmed on the ground.

Aramis laughed as he gazed at the fallen guard. "This one won't bother you again, D'Artagnan."

The Gascon was far too busy with his own battle to notice. The man from Meung, who was not as skilled as D'Artagnan, was sporting two crimson patches, one on the shoulder and the other just above the knee. Though wounded he still managed to put up a reasonable fight matching thrust to thrust with D'Artagnan.

Aramis pressed the tip of his sword downward pricking the lackey's chest. Blood flowered against his white shirt around the blade. For a single moment Aramis looked away, watching D'Artagnan subdue his opponent. It was then that the lackey grabbed a handful of dirt. When the Musketeer turned back, he threw dirt into Aramis' face, blinding him.

Aramis stepped back, pulling his sword from the lackey's chest. "You fiend!" he cried as he attempted to wipe away the blinding dirt. The lackey grabbed his blade and jumped to his feet.

"Now who has the upper hand, Monsieur?" he asked with great satisfaction.

Unable to see, Aramis swung his sword blindly through the air. "You coward!" he cried.

"Maybe," said the lackey. "No one will know but you… and you, my friend, will be dead!"

Keith leaped from the porch and hit the ground at a dead run, heading toward the guard. "Nooooo!" he cried. The lackey turned to meet the attack but it was too late, Keith lowered his shoulder and with all his might, barreled into the man's midsection.

"Oooof!" cried the lackey, sounding more like a burst tire than a man. Down on the ground he fell with Keith firmly on top. With both fists flying and soundly hitting their mark, the man struggled to throw the boy off.

"All right!" shouted Bobby as he flew over the railing, rushing to his friend's aid.

Aramis had finally cleared his eyes. Then, seeing Keith sitting atop and pummeling the lackey, a laugh escaped—loud, rolling, deep laughter. Reaching over, Aramis snatched Keith by the back of his shirt and yanked the boy off the helpless lackey. Keith's arms were still swinging wildly through the air as Aramis suspended him powerlessly above the ground. Keith quickly stopped his arms from flaying as Aramis set him down.

"What is your name?" asked Aramis as Bobby scooped

up the lackey's sword and stood next to Keith.

"A-A-Ara...," stammered Keith as his cheeks flushed. "I-I-I mean Keith, Sir."

"Well done, young Keith," said Aramis brightly. He took the sword from Bobby. "And you?"

"Uh... Bobby, Sir."

Aramis swung around and glared sharply at the fallen man. "Do not move," he growled. "If you so much as shiver, I will set these boys upon you like a pack of dogs!"

The man gave a curt nod. Then Aramis stood over the man and placed the tip of the sword within the plume of red that stained the lackey's white shirt. "Take this," he said to Keith. "If he moves I want you to run him through!"

Keith gulped loudly. "Huh?"

"Not a move, mind you," growled Aramis. "I must help my friend, D'Artagnan."

"Uh-huh," replied Keith nervously.

Aramis turned toward the fight. D'Artagnan and the man from Meung were still locked in a fierce struggle. Their swords echoed as they clashed. Bobby's heart felt as if it would explode. He couldn't imagine how Keith must feel while holding a sword to a man's chest.

"Are you okay?" asked Bobby as he gazed into his friend's eyes.

"I-I think so," he replied as he pressed the blade just a little bit harder against the lackey's chest. "This is great!"

"What?"

Keith's face split with a wide grin. His cheeks flushed even more brightly but his voice had turned calm, almost steely.

"Are you kidding, Bobby?" he said loudly. "I actually fought alongside the great Aramis!"

Bobby felt his cheeks pull his lips into a smile. He had never seen Keith like this—brave and confident. His thoughts were quickly interrupted by the sound of Aramis shouting at D'Artagnan.

"I will continue the fight, my friend," he barked. "You must go to Buckingham!"

"No!" replied D'Artagnan as he parried another thrust from his opponent "This is my score to settle!"

Aramis bent over from laughter. "I promise not to kill him, D'Artagnan. I will be happy to leave that simple task to you. Now go!"

D'Artagnan pulled away from his foe and bowed to Aramis who returned the gesture. Aramis' blade whistled through the still air. As he waved his sword, it swished three times, just missing the man from Meung. Aramis pointed his sword toward the man's heart and glared.

"Remember," said D'Artagnan. "He is mine!"

Aramis tipped his hat. "On guard!" he growled before rushing headlong toward the man from Meung.

D'Artagnan rushed to the porch. "Max!" he cried. "Get the children."

Max and Jeanne ran to Bobby and Keith. "Come on, boys. We need to go—"

Keith shook his head furiously. "I'm stayin'!" he exclaimed proudly.

Bobby stepped closer to Keith. "If Keith stays, then so do I!"

"There is little time," said D'Artagnan. "I will get the horses!"

Aramis broke away from the fight for a moment and pointed his sword toward Keith.

"Let him stay," he said. Aramis smiled. "Do not worry. He will be safe with me."

"I'm staying too!" snapped Bobby.

"You must come!" said Grandpa Max.

"No!"

Jeanne took Bobby's hand and squeezed it tightly. Bobby gazed into her sparkling eyes and sighed.

"You must come with us," she said softly, "D'Artagnan needs you…we need you…"

Bobby took in a deep breath and let it out slowly. He turned to Keith.

"Are you sure you'll be okay?" he asked.

Keith turned and looked Bobby square in the eye. "I've never felt more okay in my life." Keith's smile broadened.

As the four rode toward Calais, Bobby thought of how he would never forget his last glimpses of Keith and Aramis. Keith bravely holding the lackey at bay while Aramis' sword flashed brightly in the afternoon sun. Soon Keith and Aramis would disappear over the horizon in a cloud of dust, but not the memory of Keith truly becoming a King's Musketeer.

Chapter Seventeen
Baptiste

Bobby rested comfortably against a large oak tree. A breeze blew thin wisps of hair from his face and the leaves bristled above. He sighed. Both friends were gone—Fritzy with Porthos, Keith with Aramis. Only Athos remained. But when would he arrive? Bobby hoped it would be soon. This adventure needed to end before they damaged the book forever.

Grandpa Max plopped down next to his grandson. Bobby's mood was transparent. Max gave the young man's shoulder a firm, grandfatherly squeeze.

"Don't worry," he said softly, "Fritzy and Keith will be fine."

Bobby narrowed his eyes but didn't speak.

"Really," said his grandfather. "Porthos and Aramis will watch over them—"

"I know," snapped Bobby. "That's not the problem."

Grandpa Max shifted so he and Bobby were eye to eye. "Oh," he began softly. "You're worried about the book."

His grandson nodded.

"I am, too."

"What can we do?" pleaded Bobby. "Is it too late—?"

Grandpa Max covered Bobby's mouth with his hand. "Shhh," he hissed. "Not so loud. D'Artagnan is just over there." He shook his head. "No, I don't think it's too late, but…" Max closed his eyes.

"But what?" pressed Bobby.

"…There is a chance that the book could show some differences…"

Bobby stiffened. "Do you mean just your book…or every book of *The Three Musketeers*?"

Grandpa Max took a deep breath and exhaled slowly. His shoulders slumped in rhythm to his breath,

"I-I'm afraid all of them—"

"Do you mean *every* book?"

Max laughed nervously. "That's my guess."

Bobby jumped to his feet. "We can't let that happen!"

Grandpa Max pulled Bobby to the ground. "Shhhh!" he hissed loudly. D'Artagnan shot them a questioning glance. "Smile," continued Max without moving his lips. Bobby did. Satisfied that all was well, D'Artagnan looked away.

"Look," Grandpa Max continued, "I think that as long as we find Buckingham and get the jewels to the queen…and none of the principles in the book get killed—"

"You mean the Three Musketeers?" interrupted Bobby.

"No," replied Max. "I mean everyone. So, we can't let

D'Artagnan kill anyone important to the book."

Bobby sneered. "Oh, like that's gonna be easy!"

"We have to do it! Somehow, we've got to keep D'Artagnan from harming anyone he's not supposed to on this journey."

"Then what?" asked Bobby, who was becoming more confounded by the minute. "What happens once we get the jewels to the queen?"

"We collect Keith and Fritzy, get back to the bakery and go home."

"And everything will be fine?"

Grandpa Max didn't reply.

"You're not sure are you, Grandpa?"

Bobby's grandfather shook his head. "We can only hope, Bobby. We can only hope."

Unknown to Bobby and his grandfather, Jeanne's thoughtful eyes and ears were busy trying to discern all that they were saying. Bobby, glancing her way, noticed that he and Grandpa Max had caught her attention. He grabbed his grandfather's arm and squeezed hard.

"What—?" Max glanced at Bobby then followed the boy's gaze.

Jeanne scooted across the tall grass and settled next to Bobby.

"What are you two up to?" asked Jeanne, her voice hovering just above a whisper.

Bobby shook his head. "I can't say—"

"Or you won't," she snapped.

"Look, Jeanne—"

"No!" she cried. "You look! My father is in the Bastille, I am traveling with strangers, characters are coming and going and I'm scared to death. I heard you talking about a book. What book?"

Bobby and Grandpa Max were suddenly speechless. Jeanne had suspected that there was something wrong from the very start and they knew it.

"I think we'd better tell her," said Bobby softly. Grandpa Max nodded. Bobby looked toward D'Artagnan; the Gascon appeared to have fallen asleep.

Grandpa Max leaned toward Jeanne and in a raspy, hushed voice he explained everything. Occasionally Max would glance over at D'Artagnan to see if he was stirring. Once he was satisfied that the Gascon was still sleeping, he would continue. Grandpa Max told her about the mysterious old lady who had given him the odd box of antique books and how they actually, somehow, transported him into the books.

"And that's how we got to the point we are now," he concluded. Grandpa Max leaned back against the tree.

Jeanne narrowed her eyes. Bobby could tell she was perplexed. Finally, after a few moments of silent thought, she said, "So, what is the problem?"

Grandpa Max shot straight up. Bobby held up his hand.

"I've got this one, Grandpa," he said brightly. Then, smiling sadly at Jeanne, he said, "What we are experiencing is not *in* the book…uh…you're not *in* the book."

Jeanne tipped her head. "So?"

"So," began Bobby, "if we don't reach the same conclusion as the book, it is possible that it will be changed forever—every copy that was ever printed."

Jeanne nodded. "Then we must make it so, no?"

Bobby's shoulders slumped forward as if the air had been let out of him.

"You see," he said nervously, "You and your father aren't in *The Three Musketeers*."

"Then how did I get here?" she inquired.

Grandpa Max slowly raised his hand and said, "My fault."

"Your fault! How?"

"It seems that it was my fault that Athos, Porthos and Aramis were detained by Cardinal Richelieu."

Jeanne frowned in silence. Lines furrowed across her freckled forehead.

"Then we must make sure that the outcome is the same," she said seriously.

Bobby gripped her hand. It felt moist, sweaty. Jeanne was nervous and scared but trying not to show it.

"But that could mean that you might not exist when we do," said Grandpa Max.

Jeanne stared deeply into Bobby's blue eyes. A small smile cracked her face.

"There is no choice," she said bravely. "The book must be protected."

"But, Jeanne," snapped Bobby, "you don't understand… or you don't believe us."

Jeanne closed her eyes and let out a long sigh.

"Oh, but I do," she replied softly. "Oh, but I do—"

Jeanne's eyes widened and her face suddenly paled.

Bobby gave her a puzzled look.

"What's wrong?" he asked. Jeanne's gaze froze above Bobby's head.

"Uh-oh," said Grandpa Max.

Bobby spun around. "Baptiste!" he exclaimed.

"Aye," replied the large guard. A wide smile formed below his still swollen nose. "Now we put an end to this race—and you lose!" Baptiste drew his sword with a flourish.

Bobby turned to warn D'Artagnan but it was too late. Two dark figures stood over the helpless Gascon, their swords drawn and pressed against his chest, making small clouds of crimson form around the steel tips. Bobby's shoulders drooped in defeat.

"No one move!" warned Baptiste, as he strode toward D'Artagnan. The guard knelt down and swooped up the Gascon's sword from the ground. Baptiste inspected the handle minutely. "Ah," he continued. His tone seemed lighter, almost friendly. "I must thank you for giving me such a fine weapon, Monsieur D'Artagnan."

D'Artagnan abruptly pushed the two blades from his chest and stood. "Hand me my weapon, you coward," he snapped, "and we will settle this like men!"

Baptiste laughed loudly. "I have no doubt of your skill, Monsieur. In fact, I have no doubt of the outcome, if we *were* to fight." He pointed toward his companions. "My friends here will ensure that it is I who will walk away…and, with your sword."

Bobby leaped to his feet. "You'll have to kill me first!"

Baptiste's gaze slowly turned away from D'Artagnan

finally settling on Bobby.

"That," he said slowly, "I would enjoy."

Grandpa Max jumped between Baptiste and Bobby. "Not while I'm alive!" he exclaimed.

Baptiste laughed again before his smiling face contorted into a dark, sullen mask. He stroked his inflamed nose gently.

"Killing *you,* Monsieur," said Baptiste slowly, "I will enjoy even more."

Grandpa Max huddled Bobby and Jeanne behind him. The old man stood straight and defiant.

"I am the one you want!" shouted D'Artagnan. "I warn you. Leave the old man and children alone!"

"You warn me?" cried Baptiste incredulously. "Monsieur, you are in no position to warn anyone—"

"But I am!" shouted a voice hidden from view by the thick woods.

Baptiste and his comrades swung around in all directions looking for the intruder.

"Show yourself!" cried Baptiste. His voice cracked nervously.

A thickly built man wearing the emblem of The King's Musketeers stepped out from behind a large tree and bowed gracefully. Baptiste gasped. His henchmen trembled.

D'Artagnan smiled broadly.

"Athos!" shouted the Gascon.

Chapter Eighteen
Calais

Baptiste's eyes widened and his face paled at the very sound of Athos' name. The bulbous nosed guard froze. So did his companions.

"D-d-did you say, Athos?" asked the trembling Baptiste.

D'Artagnan smiled as he waved his arm toward his companion.

"Monsieur Baptiste," said D'Artagnan brightly, "may I introduce the greatest swordsman in all of France, His Majesty's Musketeer…Athos!"

Athos bowed again, with a flourish. "And now my ugly friend," he snapped. Athos stepped within a sword's length of Baptiste. "If you would be so kind, Monsieur, please return *that* sword to its master."

Baptiste's eyes widened as he gazed into the sword's shiny handle.

"Now!" exclaimed Athos, as the point of his sword quickly found Baptiste's Adam's apple. Baptiste tossed the sword away quickly, as if it burned his hand.

D'Artagnan bent and swept up his sword in one graceful move. He turned to Bobby, smiled and said, "This one, Baptiste, is *he* in the book?"

Bobby narrowed his eyes. "You heard us, didn't you? We thought you were asleep—"

The Gascon's smile widened. "Well?" he asked.

Bobby glanced up at Grandpa Max then back to D'Artagnan. The old man's eyes had confirmed all that Bobby needed to know.

"No!" exclaimed the boy. "Baptiste is not in the book."

"Then," said D'Artagnan, "I shall kill him."

Baptiste stumbled backward away from Athos' blade. "Kill me! W-what book—"

Athos stepped between D'Artagnan and Baptiste.

"What book do you refer to my friend?" Athos asked.

"Stand aside Athos," snapped D'Artagnan, "while I skewer our ugly friend here."

Athos shrugged then turned to face Baptiste's companions.

"If you must," Athos said grimly. "Then do it quickly—"

"No!" shouted Bobby.

D'Artagnan turned toward the boy. "But you said he wasn't in the book."

"Please do not kill him, Monsieur," pleaded Jeanne.

"I am very confused," confessed Athos. "Can we just

dispatch this rabble and make for Calais?"

D'Artagnan smiled broadly at his friend and said, "Agreed!" He turned back toward Baptiste. "You may dispatch the lackeys while I skewer our red nosed friend here."

Athos rushed headlong at the two guards. Swords quickly crossed and the screech of steel against steel ripped through the sunny afternoon.

D'Artagnan's sword flashed at Baptiste, forcing his back against a thick tree. The villain stumbled, but righted himself just in time to parry the Gascon's playful thrust. Flashes of sunlight reflected off their blades as their swords quickened.

Grandpa Max pushed Bobby and Jeanne toward the horses. "Get ready to mount up," he said urgently. "We might have to leave in a hurry." Bobby could sense the excitement in his grandfather's voice.

"On guard!" yelled Athos at his unworthy opponents. "Where did you learn to fight, in a convent?" With a quick thrust, one of the guards fell to one knee pressing his gloved hand on his bleeding thigh. Athos slashed at the air over the fallen man's head before turning on the other guard. In an instant the fight was over, the second guard lay flat on his back, clutching his right shoulder.

"Wow!" cried Bobby. "That was amazing!"

With a mighty swing, D'Artagnan had knocked the sword from Baptiste's hand. When the guard bent to pick up his weapon, the Gascon slapped Baptiste's backside with the edge of his blade.

"The devil!" swore Baptiste.

D'Artagnan placed the tip of his sword against Baptiste's throat. A tiny crimson thread formed beneath the blade.

"Come, D'Artagnan," snapped Athos. "Stop playing around and finish the rascal!"

Baptiste shut his eyes tightly, bravely waiting for the end.

"No!" cried Jeanne.

"D'Artagnan, stop!" exclaimed Bobby.

The Gascon gazed at the children. "But he is not in the book…"

"I know," said Bobby trying to remain calm. "Please don't kill him."

"Please," Jeanne pleaded.

"What book?" snapped Athos.

"Later, Athos!" D'Artagnan sighed loudly. "Turn around, Baptiste."

The guard obeyed. D'Artagnan shot Bobby and Jeanne a wink before striking Baptiste on the head with the handle of his sword. Baptiste hit the ground with a thud.

"Sweet dreams, my friend," said the Gascon as he sheathed his blade. "Come, let us head for Calais. We should be there within the hour."

"What book!" queried Athos again.

"LATER!" D'Artagnan, Bobby, Grandpa Max and Jeanne cried in unison.

The path to Calais was clear. In the lead, Athos thundered down the dirt road followed by Grandpa Max,

Jeanne and Bobby. D'Artagnan brought up the rear. Great clouds of dust filled the road behind them as they sped toward the seaport.

As Calais grew closer, the road wound its way through villages so small that one could miss them in the blink of an eye.

"I smell the sea!" shouted Athos, but his voice was lost amongst the sound of twenty hoofs beating against the dry earth. Athos pulled up hard on his reins, causing his horse to come to a sliding stop. The others followed in turn.

"What is it?" asked D'Artagnan as he eyed the road ahead.

"Calais, my young friend!" cried Athos loudly. "Let us make the docks before dark."

The final leg of the journey took them through a densely populated part of the seaport. Stone buildings lined the street, casting dark shadows across its dirty bricks. The horses' hoofs clip-clopped loudly, echoing along the way. Grizzled old men stepped out of dark doorways and eyed the small group suspiciously.

Bobby felt fearful. These townsmen were a nasty looking group.

"What's with these guys?" he asked Athos who tipped his hat and smiled at each and every character that they passed.

"It is my uniform," he replied. "They do not see it very often in Calais." Athos continued waving and tipping his hat to the populace. "Sometimes, I believe that the people of this country do not trust the King, or his Musketeers—"

"Athos!" called out D'Artagnan. "They seem to be

looking at you."

"I know," replied Athos. "It is the uniform, I should have changed—"

Athos was interrupted when his horse stopped dead in its tracks.

"What is this?" cried Athos.

"Wow!" exclaimed Bobby.

"What is it?" inquired D'Artagnan as he pulled his horse up next to his companions. "Mon Dieu!"

Bobby rubbed his eyes hard, hoping to wipe the vision away. He opened them slowly, but it was no use. It was still there. Blocking the path was the biggest man he had ever seen, dressed in the same black leather outfit as Baptiste and the others. He stood eye to eye with Athos' horse, the black leather patch over his left eye made his already massive build even more intimidating. The giant did not appear happy.

"*That* is the biggest man I've ever seen!" exclaimed Athos.

"That is the biggest *anything* I've ever seen!" agreed D'Artagnan.

"What should we do?" asked Bobby.

"Maybe we can talk with him," said Grandpa Max.

"*If* he can talk," replied D'Artagnan.

Athos waved at the giant and smiled. The monster did not move a muscle.

"Away with you, Monsieur," snapped Athos. "You are blocking our way!"

The giant did not move.

Athos narrowed his eyes. "In the name of the King—

get out of our way!"

The monster stood his ground.

"What should we do?" inquired Bobby.

"Go around!" exclaimed Athos. But when he turned his horse's head to the right, the monster moved to his left. Athos pulled up on the reins and urged his horse to the left. With a monstrous step, the giant moved to the right, matching the horse's movement.

"Hmmm," commented Athos. "I guess I will have to run the scamp over—"

Before Athos could finish, the monster grabbed Athos' horse by the bit. The giant's eyes narrowed and his forehead furrowed deeply. The horse tried to break free from the man's huge paw (it was certainly bigger than any human hand that any of them had ever seen) but the poor beast did not have the strength. The giant grunted loudly.

Athos gasped then turned toward D'Artagnan. "I guess I have no other choice but to fight this brute," he said nervously.

"I am not so sure it would be a fight," said D'Artagnan cautiously eyeing the giant.

"He *is* a man."

"Are you sure?" asked Bobby, looking into the monster's steely eyes.

"All of you make for the docks," replied Athos. "I will handle this."

Athos threw his leg over his horse's head and dropped onto the cobblestones, his boots landing with a sharp crack. Smiling broadly, he drew his sword and squared off with the beast.

"Well, my large friend," he said as if he were quite satisfied with the situation, "I hope that you are prepared to feel the cold steel of my—"

Before Athos could finish, the monster had snatched the sword from Athos' grip and broke it in half across his enormous leg.

"The devil!" cried Athos.

In his surprise, D'Artagnan's eyes widened as big as saucers. "Do you still want us to leave?" he asked sheepishly.

Athos did not answer at first.

"Uh…y-yes…go!" he finally replied.

"Good luck, my friend," said D'Artagnan.

"Thank you," replied Athos nervously. "I am going to need it!"

"I'm staying to help Athos!" declared Bobby bravely.

"No!" exclaimed D'Artagnan.

"We can't just leave him—"

Grandpa Max reached out for Bobby's shoulder. "You go," he said. "I'll stay and help Athos!"

"But Grandpa, what will you—?"

Bobby's grandfather tapped his temple with a bony finger. "I still have a trick or two up my sleeve."

"GO!" screamed Athos. "Go before the ferry leaves without you!" The giant had reached out and grabbed poor Athos' face. He was smothered by the monster's grip.

Jeanne pulled at D'Artagnan's sleeve. "Come. I will show you the way to the ferry."

Athos managed a muffled scream. "GO!"

"Go!" cried Grandpa Max as he leaped from his horse.

Bobby and the others rode away at a full gallop. As the boy glanced over his shoulder, he shuddered at the sight of the monster holding the kicking, screaming Athos high over his head. Grandpa Max's fists pounded feverishly at the giant's chest. It was not a pretty sight. Tears formed in his young eyes. He certainly hoped that it would not be the last time that he ever saw his Grandpa Max or Athos again.

Chapter Nineteen
As Luck Would Have It

The salty night air felt cool and damp against Bobby's skin. There were no stars as darkness enveloped the small ship that D'Artagnan had engaged to cross the English Channel. Bobby focused on the only good things he could think of –at least the sea was remaining calm and so was his stomach.

The tiny ship had cast off and the lights from shore began to dim. Bobby, numbed with fear, couldn't help worrying if Grandpa Max was safe or if they would all make it back safely to Sky Harbor.

Then, as a small tear rolled slowly down his cheek, Bobby felt a warm hand envelop his. It was Jeanne.

"Do not worry," she said brightly, attempting to cheer him up. "Monsieur Max will be fine—I am sure."

Bobby turned to Jeanne. Her eyes sparkled brightly against the ship's dim lamps.

"I can't help it, Jeanne," he said softly. "He's my grandfather and he might really be in trouble…"

Bobby's voice trailed off as he watched the sparkle in Jeanne's eyes fade.

"…I-I'm sorry," he continued, "I forgot about your dad being in the Bastille—"

Jeanne spun away. "I cannot bear to think of him being in that awful place." She sobbed loudly. "The Bastille is a prison like no other. I have heard people speak of lashings and horrible torture—"

"Don't worry. D'Artagnan and his friends will free him!"

"If he and the others are even still alive," she replied. Jeanne continued to sob. "If my father is still alive—"

"Stop!" exclaimed Bobby. "I'm sure it will all be okay…I mean…" He felt his heart sink. "…I don't know what I mean. I just know that everything will be okay."

Jeanne leaned toward Bobby and kissed him gently on the cheek. His face flushed warmly. Bobby was glad it was dark so Jeanne wouldn't notice his reddened cheeks.

"Thank you," whispered Jeanne.

"F-for what?" inquired a confused Bobby.

Jeanne shrugged and smiled. "I am not really sure. But I think that, somehow, we both feel better now."

And they did.

The trip across the channel was less than eventful. The sailors who manned the small vessel were efficient and polite. One older seaman had been very helpful as poor Jeanne had come down with a bad case of sea sickness. Upon noticing

Jeanne's frowning, pale face, the old sailor went quickly below and within a few moments reappeared on deck with a large, sugar covered biscuit.

"Here, Lass," he said in a thick Scottish brogue. "Have a wee bit of this, it'll make that gut of yours feel a whole lot better."

Jeanne didn't understand, but she turned green at the sight of the sugary bread. "But...I cannot..." She turned away quickly raising a hand to cover her mouth.

The old man smiled. "I know," he chuckled, "the sight of food on a sour stomach be hard to take, but give it a try, Lass, I swear you'll be feelin' better in no time at all."

With Bobby's urging, Jeanne finally took a small bite and managed to force it down. She took another bite and another until her eyes began to sparkle again. Jeanne smiled widely at the old sailor.

"Don' mention it, Lass. It works every time."

"Land ho!" cried a voice from the darkness above.

"Ah," said the old man. "I've got to go back to me work now."

Before the old man could turn away, Jeanne threw her arms around his neck and kissed him on the cheek. The old man chuckled as he walked away.

The sun had finally risen and the smell of the fires from the night before still lingered in the city's heavy air. The sounds of horse drawn carriages and merchants calling out in hopes of selling their wares filled the streets and alleyways.

D'Artagnan had no idea where he might find the Duke

of Buckingham. It was his first time in England and London was such a large and busy place. Worst of all, the Gascon knew not a word of English. D'Artagnan tried to show people on the street the letter that he was to deliver to the Duke, but no one would stop, especially for a stranger who spoke French. Frustrated, he sat at the edge of a small fountain. The water trickled lazily behind him.

"I am afraid it is no use," he said gloomily. D'Artagnan was beginning to show signs of exhaustion. "I have failed my Queen."

Bobby sat beside him. "Maybe I can help."

D'Artagnan narrowed one eye. "How can this be? You do not speak English—"

"It's too hard to explain," replied Bobby. "But if my hunch is right, I think I can track down the Duke for you."

D'Artagnan and Jeanne shot each other a puzzled glance. Finally, the Gascon shrugged and pressed the letter from the Queen of France into Bobby's waiting hand.

"Stay here," Bobby continued, "I'll be right back."

Bobby had one hope as he walked from the fountain, that when he spoke in London, it would be heard as English and not French. He approached a portly looking gentleman with a large balding head and adorned in bright robes.

"Excuse me," Bobby offered politely. The man looked at him strangely. All would be lost if no one could understand him. He held out the folded letter and tried again. "Excuse me, sir,' he continued, "Could you possibly tell me where the Duke of Buckingham lives. We really need to deliver this letter to him."

The man smiled incredulously at the boy, but didn't say a word. Bobby was certain that he must still sound as if he were speaking French. He shrugged.

"Sorry, Mister," he said softly then began to walk away. "I didn't mean to bo—"

"From where have you come, boy?" snapped the portly gentleman. Bobby swung around in an instant.

"You understood me?"

The man laughed heartily, his stout belly shook beneath his red robes. "Of course I can understand you," he said loudly. "But, I must admit to not being familiar with your strange accent. Are you from the North?"

Bobby started to shake his head, but it quickly turned into a nod.

"I thought so," said the man. "As to the Duke of Buckingham," the man pointed toward a large palace just down the street, "he resides there."

"Great!" cried Bobby. "Thank you. Thank you so much—"

"I am afraid that you will not find him, though." The man continued graciously. "I myself have just left there and the Duke is hunting with the King."

"But, we must see the Duke!"

The man glanced at D'Artagnan and Jeanne who sat patiently at the fountain's edge. Looking back at Bobby, he sighed.

"What is so important that you must see the Duke of Buckingham?"

"I can't tell you, but it is really, really important—"

"Who are your companions?" inquired the man. "They appear to be French."

"They are—"

"Why would a Frenchman need to see the Duke of Buckingham?"

"B-but, how could you know he was French?"

The portly figure laughed with a jolly roar then replied, "Ah, but I am a man of the world *and* the Duke's secretary—"

"His secretary?" howled Bobby. "Wait right here!" Bobby started toward the fountain then suddenly turned back toward the man. "You're sure that you're the Duke's secretary?"

The man nodded and smiled.

"The Duke of Buckingham's secretary?"

"None other," replied the man.

"Whoopee!" cried Bobby as he waved his arms feverishly to D'Artagnan.

D'Artagnan could not have looked more relieved as their new friend spoke French. The Gascon explained the situation, even going as far as to show the man the Queen of France's seal that was on the letter.

"Come with me, right away," said the man as he led the way toward the palace. "This must be extremely important if signed by the Queen of France herself."

"You have no idea," stated D'Artagnan. "The fates of both our countries lie within that folded scrap of paper."

The duke's secretary placed the letter into D'Artagnan's hand. "Then the Duke must see it for himself!" With a simple wave of a hand from the secretary, the brightly dressed soldiers guarding the entrance to Buckingham Palace let them pass. Bobby, D'Artagnan and Jeanne were getting closer to completing their mission.

Chapter Twenty
The Cardinal and the Duke

"**W**hat book?" inquired an impatient Richelieu.

Baptiste shifted his weight backward, as if trying to escape the cardinal's question. "I'm not sure, Your Eminence," he replied hesitantly. "B-b-but I do remember the boy saying something about me not being in it—"

"Of course, of course," said the Cardinal. "Go on man, tell me more!"

Baptiste felt as if he would wilt and blow away at any second. He had always feared Cardinal Richelieu and His Eminence's apparent bad mood didn't make things any easier

"I-I'm afraid that I do not know…" he replied softly. "D'Artagnan asked the old man and the boy if I was in the book…" Baptiste paused briefly as Richelieu's eyes narrowed. "…When the boy told the Gascon I was not, he threatened to kill me."

"But yet, you are still alive," countered Richelieu. "Why did the rascal not take your life?"

"The children stopped him, Your Eminence—"

"This book, no doubt, possesses information about the Queen and Buckingham."

"But... Your Eminence—"

"I want that book!" exclaimed the Cardinal. "Do not fail me again, Baptiste!"

"But, Your Eminence, what of D'Artagnan and the jewels?"

Richelieu leaned back in his chair; his raised eyebrow gave him a sinister appearance. Baptiste nearly shuddered out loud. "You let me worry about that. You bring me that book!"

"B-but I have not seen this book—"

"Silence!" shouted Richelieu. "Now go!"

Baptiste backed quickly toward the open door, bowing hesitantly before disappearing like a thief into the dark hallway. Baptiste's steps had barely faded when a dark figure stepped out from behind the curtains and placed his hand upon the back of the Cardinal's chair.

"The young Gascon would seem quite resourceful, Your Eminence," he said sharply.

Richelieu looked into the stranger's dark, piercing stare. "I had hoped that Baptiste would eliminate him."

"Baptiste is a bumbling fool," laughed the stranger. "I shall deal with the Gascon myself." Then, as if staring into his own thoughts, he growled, "Had I known the trouble this young rascal would cause, I would have killed him when I first laid eyes on him in Meung."

"That would have been wise, Rochefort," agreed the Cardinal. "Are you sure that you can kill him now?"

"What!" grumbled Rochefort.

"You barely escaped Aramis' blade—"

"But, Your Eminence, I would have killed him but for—"

Richelieu cut Rochefort off with a curt wave of the hand. "No more of this."

"What of this book?" asked the man from Meung.

"Ha," laughed Richelieu. "A fool's chase for our friend Baptiste."

Rochefort stroked his narrow mustache. "This book interests me, Your Eminence."

"All I care about is that it keeps Baptiste out of your way." The Cardinal reached into a small drawer of his desk and removed a small pouch. "Here is enough gold to cover any costs it may take to stop this Gascon. The jewels must not reach Paris!"

Rochefort turned to leave.

"Oh, and Rochefort?"

"Yes, Your Eminence," he said turning to gaze into the Cardinal's old, steely eyes.

"Do not fail!"

"It shall be done, Your Eminence."

As Rochefort quickly disappeared into the hallway, Richelieu leaned back in his chair and tented his bony fingers beneath his nose.

"It had better," he whispered to an empty room.

Before long, Bobby, D'Artagnan and Jeanne were in a

well appointed carriage, racing through the English countryside.
The dark green of the forest greatly contrasted with the gray,
clouded sky. The road, filled with deep weathered holes,
caused the carriage to bump and rock along the way. Luckily,
the trip was short.

D'Artagnan stared hopefully through the coach's
window as it pulled to a rocking stop near a small clearing in
the trees. The Gascon threw the door open and landed on the
ground with a loud thud.

"I hope Buckingham remembers me," D'Artagnan said
to Bobby.

"He will," replied the boy. "Just don't mistake him
for Aramis again—" Bobby stopped suddenly realizing
what he had read in the book. D'Artagnan had mistaken the
Duke of Buckingham for Aramis as he left the palace with
D'Artagnan's beloved Constance Bonacieux, Her Majesty's
maid and confidant. Buckingham, who loved the Queen dearly,
had dressed as one of His Majesty's Musketeers to gain entry
to the palace. Being very jealous and completely unaware that
Constance was escorting the Duke away from a clandestine
appointment with Her Majesty, D'Artagnan realized the man
was not Aramis and challenged Buckingham to a duel.

D'Artagnan narrowed his eyes at the boy. "How could
you know this…?" A thin smile spread below his narrow
mustache. "…Ah, the book!"

Bobby smiled back.

Buckingham's secretary piled out of the coach and he
and D'Artagnan started for the woods.

"Stay in the coach until I return!" shouted the Gascon,

just before disappearing behind a small clump of brush.

Only a few minutes had passed before D'Artagnan and the secretary had made their way back to the small clearing. Joining them was a strongly built, handsome man, no more than thirty-five years old. He walked with great authority—like a proud soldier.

"That must be him," said Bobby softly.

"Oh," replied Jeanne, "he is so handsome—even more so than D'Artagnan."

Bobby felt a sudden twinge of jealousy, but it quickly disappeared as the men climbed into the carriage.

"Children?" inquired the duke with a raised brow.

D'Artagnan glanced toward Bobby and Jeanne and said, "I will explain on the way. But let me say that without the help of these children and two others, I would not be here to serve you and the Queen."

"Don't forget Grandpa Max!" exclaimed Bobby.

"And Athos, Porthos and Aramis!" added Jeanne.

As the carriage jerked and began to roll away, Buckingham turned to D'Artagnan and asked, "How much time before you must leave so the Queen has the jewels for the ball?"

"Three days M'Lord," replied the Gascon.

Buckingham stroked his chin thoughtfully. "That should be enough time for my jeweler to make the copies… with a little persuasion." The Duke laughed. "Do not worry. I promise you, my young friend, we will not let Her Majesty down."

* * *

Buckingham was a man of his word. On the third day Bobby, D'Artagnan and Jeanne were sailing across the channel in possession of the two gems. The Gascon leaned against the rail at the ship's narrow bow.

"D'Artagnan?" said Bobby as he approached. D'Artagnan glanced over his shoulder. "What about my grandfather and Fritzy and Keith? I'm really worried about them."

The Gascon threw his head back and chuckled. "Do not worry, my young friend. Max and the boys are in good hands."

"But—"

"My comrades are the bravest and best in all of France... maybe the world."

Bobby nodded, but the Gascon could tell that the boy was not convinced. D'Artagnan grasped the boy's shoulder and squeezed it affectionately.

"Seriously, Bobby," said D'Artagnan softly. "Have no fear. Your friends will be fine."

Waiting upon the ship's arrival in Calais were D'Artagnan's faithful lackey, Planchet, and four saddled horses.

"Ah, Planchet," cried D'Artagnan brightly. "How did you know that we would only need three horses?"

"I didn't," replied the lackey. "They were all I could afford."

D'Artagnan laughed heartily as he sprung up onto his mount.

"Are we going to look for Grandpa Max and my friends along the way?" asked Bobby as he climbed up on his mount.

D'Artagnan shook his head. "There is no time. We must get to Paris. Once that is done we will come back for the others."

"But—"

"Do not fear, Bobby," began D'Artagnan, "Planchet will stay behind to look for them."

"May I stay to help Planchet?" inquired Jeanne. "I know the area better than he."

D'Artagnan glanced toward his lackey. Planchet nodded.

"Good," continued D'Artagnan. "Come Bobby, we are off to Paris."

Bobby gazed inquiringly into Jeanne's bright eyes.

"Go," she said, softly reassuring him. "I will be fine with Planchet.

"Give Grandpa Max a hug for me when you find him."

Bobby and D'Artagnan turned their mounts and sped into Calais. Bobby couldn't help thinking about Grandpa Max and his friends as he followed D'Artagnan from the docks. He also couldn't help thinking about how much damage they had probably caused to one of the greatest books ever written.

Chapter Twenty One
The Man from Meung

Curiously, the trip to Paris was uneventful. Barely a soul passed on the road as Bobby and D'Artagnan sped through the beautiful French countryside.

"We must ride for twelve hours, my young friend!" D'Artagnan shouted over the thundering hoofs. "Can you do it?"

Bobby nodded. "What about the horses?"

D'Artagnan shook his head. "We will find new mounts halfway!"

So on they rode. As the hours passed, Bobby grew tired and his backside ached. But he said nothing. He wouldn't complain. Bobby knew how important this mission was to D'Artagnan, the Queen and France. After six grueling hours on the road, they stopped at a small village and headed directly for the town livery.

The blacksmith was a jovial type. He had a large, dirty

face and a genuine smile. After some negotiations, the smith agreed to take their horses and a small pouch of gold for two fresh mounts. The way was clear to Paris. After a quick stop at a local inn for some biscuits and milk, Bobby and D'Artagnan were off.

The hours felt like days to Bobby. The seat of his pants had never felt so sore. But up ahead, in the soft light of dusk, there was hope. The buildings of Paris grew larger with every mile. The smells and sounds of the great city were more than welcome to the weary riders. But still, Bobby was confused as to the complete absence of Richelieu's guards.

"There!" cried D'Artagnan. "There is the palace!"

Bobby's heart leapt. He was exhausted, hungry and most of all, blistered.

D'Artagnan pulled up hard on the reins bringing his horse to a skidding stop in front of a tall vine covered wall. Bobby did the same.

"We must get into the palace," hissed D'Artagnan. "I fear that we might be too late. The ballet has already started. Hold the horses, Bobby. I will climb the wall—"

"You are correct, Gascon," said a darkly dressed man who appeared from the shadows. "You are too late." The man drew his sword. "The ballet has indeed started and the Queen will soon appear before the King, most inconveniently bereft of the jewels she gave to Buckingham."

"You again!" spat D'Artagnan. "My man from Meung!"

The man bowed from the waist with a flourish.

"You have no lackeys to attack me this time," continued D'Artagnan as he drew his sword. "On guard!"

"Ah," said Rochefort confidently. "You are correct, my young friend. I do not have my lackey's this time."

"Then it is just you and I—"

"Not quite!" exclaimed the man. His dark eyes glistened with anticipation. "I do not have my lackeys…but, I do have four of the Cardinal Richelieu's finest swordsman."

Bobby gasped as four men dressed in black stepped from the shadows. *The Cardinal's Guard!*

"I would think," continued Rochefort, "that I have the better odds. Wouldn't you?"

D'Artagnan, his shoulders slumped, sighed with sad exasperation. He couldn't speak. Bobby knew how exhausted the Gascon was—he was terribly fatigued as well. They had come so far and so close to completing the mission—to save his Queen and possibly France.

"I believe," boomed a deep voice from behind, "that the odds have just improved!"

"Porthos!" cried Bobby. Then he saw a small figure step from behind the giant musketeer. "Fritzy!"

D'Artagnan swung around and grinned. His energy renewed, he stepped toward Rochefort.

"The devil!" shouted Rochefort. "Two men and two boys—"

"The devil, yourself!" snapped another voice—this one from across the cobblestone street. "Three men and three boys!"

"Aramis!" exclaimed D'Artagnan.

"Keith!" cried Bobby.

"You are wrong!" called out another voice with authority. "We are four musketeers and three, wee musketeers!"

It was Athos *and* Grandpa Max.

Bobby looked again at Fritzy and Keith; his friends wore their homemade King's Musketeer uniforms. Fritzy rushed to Bobby's side and handed him his white plumed hat, coverlet and his trusty wooden sword. He quickly pulled on the shirt and hat.

"Now," cried Porthos brightly, "We are ready!" He held his sword to the sky and shouted, "ALL FOR ONE!"

"ONE FOR ALL!" answered the King's Musketeers—men *and* boys.

Athos, Porthos and Aramis rushed the guards as D'Artagnan and Rochefort crossed swords. Athos and Aramis took on one swordsman each as the massive Porthos fell upon the other two. There was a great clashing of steel. Blades flashed brightly against the rising light of the street lamps. The boys looked on in amazement as the skilled combatants exacted steel against steel. But Porthos began to struggle against his two adversaries.

"Grandpa Max, What can we do?" cried Bobby.

"See if you can help Porthos!" he replied.

Bobby turned toward the fight. Grandpa Max grabbed him by the collar.

"Remember, Do not!" exclaimed Grandpa Max. "I repeat, *do not* let D'Artagnan or anyone kill Rochefort! If he dies the book could be ruined forever!"

Bobby nodded. Then, narrowing his eyes at Fritzy and Keith, he raised his sword to the sky.

"Musketeers!" he cried. The others raised their swords. "Let's go!"

The boys rushed toward Porthos.

"Let's get him!" cried Keith, his sword ready for battle.

"Geronimo!" screamed Fritzy while at a full run.

Bobby reached the fourth guard first and skillfully slid by his waving blade. He wrapped his arms around the man's legs. Porthos' eyes widened as he watched Fritzy and Keith barrel head first into the guard's stomach, forcing him to trip over Bobby and fall helplessly to the street. Bobby jumped to his feet and with one mighty kick, sent the man's sword flying into the shadows. Meanwhile, Fritzy and Keith jumped up and down on the man's chest. He cried for mercy.

With a great flurry of swords, Porthos disarmed his foe. Within seconds Athos and Aramis had done the same. The only fight that raged on was the one between D'Artagnan and the man from Meung.

Rochefort was a far better swordsman than D'Artagnan could have imagined. The villain matched the Gascon blow for blow, thrust for thrust and parry for parry; neither could gain the advantage. Even in the absence of his companions and surrounded by King's Musketeers, the man from Meung fought as if ice water ran through his veins. But the Gascon gained the advantage.

With an astonishing ballet move, D'Artagnan spun into the air, barely avoiding a Rochefort thrust. The man from Meung stumbled forward and when the Gascon landed he brought the edge of his sword down hard upon the man's wrist. Rochefort dropped his sword and stepped away. Blood dripped onto the rough stones, glistening black in the dim street light.

Finally, with his back against the wall, Rochefort

dropped to his knees to accept his fate. "Kill me quickly, young Gascon!" he exclaimed in defiance.

D'Artagnan pressed his blade against Rochefort's throat. A tiny trickle of blood stained his collar. The man from Meung closed his eyes. His men who were being held by Porthos gasped as they watched their leader prepare to die. The Gascon's eyes turned to steel, his jaw trembled with anger.

"Stop!" cried Bobby. "You can't"—

"I must!" exclaimed D'Artagnan.

"But the book!"

"I do not care about the book, Bobby," he growled. "I must have my revenge!"

Suddenly, there was a flash of steel and D'Artagnan's blade whipped up and away from Rochefort's throat.

"Not today, my young friend!" exclaimed Athos pointing toward a small gate that broke up the tall, blank wall. "Look!"

D'Artagnan wheeled around as the gate opened and a small woman wearing a hooded cape appeared on the street.

"Constance," he gasped.

"Come quickly," said a sweet, calming voice. "It is not too late. The Queen awaits you."

D'Artagnan turned and glared at Rochefort and said, "It would seem as if this were your lucky day. Enjoy what is left— it may still yet be your last."

"Go!" cried Athos.

"Go!" echoed Bobby, Fritzy and Keith.

D'Artagnan glanced at his friends and the boys and smiled. Then, bringing his sword up in front of his face, he bowed.

"Thank you all," he said brightly, before disappearing with Constance into the palace.

Chapter Twenty-Two
Going Home

Xavier rushed from the bakery out into the dark street.
D'Artagnan, Athos, Porthos, Aramis, Max and the boys should
have been back long before now. The baker leaned up against
the streetlight. Pacing inside the bakery had become tiring; it
felt far better to be out in the fresh air.

While Xavier's eyes searched the dark street, a shady
figure slithered unseen inside the bakery door. Moving quickly,
the man snuck into the kitchen. He sighed. *It was certainly
a large place,* he thought, but Cardinal Richelieu wanted
the book and Baptiste had no intention of disappointing His
Eminence.

A glance around at the ovens and pans quickly revealed
the book was nowhere in sight. Baptiste wasn't even certain of
what he was looking for. But that wasn't important, time was
short. He pushed on into the back room. Luckily, Xavier had lit
a candle, and the flickering light provided more than enough to

continue his search.

Baptiste narrowed his eyes as he surveyed the bakery's back room. The shelves were filled with flour and more baking pans filled the walls. He began to search. One by one, Baptiste removed the bags of flour to see if the book might be hidden behind them. The white powder filled the air as he laid each sack back into its proper place.

On and on, he continued his search until his uniform and face were completely covered in floury white. Once Baptiste realized how funny he must look, he proceeded to dust himself off.

Frustrated that the book had not shown up during his search, he stopped to think. Baptiste casually leaned against another cabinet of shelves—it moved! He gathered himself up quickly and put his shoulder into it. It moved again. Baptiste could barely contain his excitement; this must be where the book was hidden. He pushed again. Stairs!

"That crafty baker!" he cried.

Baptiste grabbed the candle and headed down the stairs. He hadn't gone three steps before the sound of voices echoed from the front of the bakery. With great haste, Baptiste disappeared beneath the floor.

"I will never forget the look on Rochefort's face as he and his great swordsmen ran from the palace!" exclaimed Porthos as he held the bakery door open for the others.

"Yeah!" cried Fritzy. "That was really cool!"

"Cool?" questioned Aramis. "Are you cold, my little musketeer?"

"I will turn on the ovens," said Xavier rushing toward

the kitchen. "That will warm you."

"No, no!" exclaimed Fritzy. "I'm not cold. I meant—" he stopped abruptly upon feeling Bobby's elbow dig deep into his side. "Ow!"

"Let it go, Fritzy," said Bobby softly.

Fritzy nodded.

Grandpa Max rubbed his thin upper arms. "Anyway, I could do with a bit of warming up."

Xavier slipped back into the front room. "Who is hungry?" he asked.

Porthos' eyes doubled in size. "Food? Did someone mention food? Have you any Spanish wine, good baker?"

Athos and Aramis laughed loudly as they slapped their hands against the much larger Porthos' shoulders and led him into the kitchen. Bobby and the others stayed behind.

"Grandpa Max," whispered Bobby, "did we fix the book?"

Bobby's grandfather rubbed the gray stubble on his chin.

"Well," he began thoughtfully, "I don't believe that anyone died…and the Queen did get the jewels in time to fool the King and the Cardinal Richelieu…"

"Well?" pressed Fritzy.

"Do you think we did it?" asked Keith.

Grandpa Max's face slowly spread into a wide smile. He nodded enthusiastically.

"I think that as long as nothing else happens, we can go home and all will be well with, *The Three Musketeers*. Come, let's join the others; D'Artagnan should be here any minute."

"Yeah," said Fritzy. "I sure could go for one of Xavier's cream puffs!"

It wasn't long before D'Artagnan joined them at the large table in Xavier's kitchen. The Gascon was all smiles as he told of his audience with the Queen.

"That must have been some audience," commented Athos while pointing mischievously at D'Artagnan's hand.

"Oh that…" replied the blushing Gascon, as he caressed the large diamond that sat atop an extraordinarily sized golden ring, "…A gift from Her Majesty."

"I'd wager that is worth quite a lot of money," observed Porthos.

"Aye," added Aramis.

"Wow!" exclaimed Bobby while eying the ring. "The Queen gave you that?"

D'Artagnan nodded.

"Do we get anything?" inquired Fritzy.

D'Artagnan stared silently at the boy.

"Well, we did help, didn't we?"

Bobby shoved Fritzy so hard that he slipped from his chair and landed on the floor. After a brief awkward silence, everyone, including Fritzy, started to laugh.

"So Max," said D'Artagnan as the laughter died down, "how is the book?"

Grandpa Max rose from his chair and held a large, gooey cream puff over the table as if he were about to give a toast and said, "To D'Artagnan and The Three Musketeers. All for one and one for all!" he took a big bite of the puff and smiled. "I believe that the book will be fine."

"Bravo!" cried D'Artagnan, Bobby and the others.

Grandpa Max's smile turned to a frown. "But, my friends, I believe that the boys and I have overstayed our welcome."

"Nonsense!" cried Porthos.

"No, no," continued Max. "We must go."

"Aw, c'mon, Grandpa Max," pleaded Bobby.

"Yeah," added Fritzy, "I want to stay and learn more from Porthos."

Aramis turned to Porthos. "So, what *have* you been teaching this boy while we were not watching?"

Porthos' face flushed crimson. "Oh…nothing in particular—"

"So you say!" exclaimed Athos and everyone started to laugh again.

"No, really," said Max, "We must be going."

"I don't want to go," snapped Keith.

"Weren't you the one who had to be home by five?"

Keith frowned. "I guess…"

"Okay then," snapped the old man, "We must go, and soon, before anything else happens." Grandpa Max stood, arms folded tightly across his chest. "Now where did I put my glasses?" he asked himself absently.

"I think you left them downstairs," said Keith between bites of cream puff.

Grandpa Max smiled. "Okay boys, you finish your snack while I go downstairs."

Max headed for the back room. Stepping through the

door he shouted, "Xavier, do you have a candle? It's dark in here."

Xavier paused, his expression showing surprise. "But, Monsieur Max, he said suspiciously, "I distinctly remember lighting a candle in there before I went outside."

"It must have blown out. Do you have another?"

"In a moment." Xavier rushed to a small cabinet and snatched a short candle in a small brass holder. He stopped by the fire to light it and handed it to Max who waited patiently by the door.

Grandpa Max turned into the back room as the moving candle flickered odd shadows against the dimly lit wall. Upon reaching the cabinet of shelves that covered the stairway, he noticed it had already been pushed aside revealing the steps. Max shrugged his shoulders, thinking that Xavier must have left the stairs uncovered in case he and the kids needed to hide from Richelieu's guards. Without another thought he started down.

Meanwhile the boys and their new friends were saying their goodbyes. Keith actually shed a tear upon telling Aramis that being with him was his greatest experience ever. Fritzy and Porthos laughed and ate more cream puffs—probably more than they should have. Bobby thanked Athos for his help in Calais, but even though he always played at being Athos, his real affection was for D'Artagnan.

"Will you tell the others after we've gone?" Bobby asked the Gascon.

"Tell them what?"

"Everything about the book," replied Bobby.

"They know enough," said D'Artagnan playfully. "A few glasses of Spanish wine and Porthos will probably forget the entire adventure." The Gascon smiled. "And besides, if Max is correct, once you have left it will start all over again and we will remember nothing."

Bobby shook his head sadly. "Grandpa Max is probably right; it will be as if we were never here."

"You look sad, my young friend."

Bobby glanced toward the bakery's front door.

"Ah," continued D'Artagnan, "You wanted to say farewell to Jeanne."

Bobby nodded glancing again at the door. "Yeah," he said softly, "I kinda did."

"Fear not, Bobby. My lackey Planchet will let no harm come to the girl. She will be here soon and we will arrange for her father's freedom from the Bastille."

Bobby let out a long sigh. "I guess you're right—" He was quickly interrupted as Grandpa Max burst into the room, a darkly dressed figure just behind him. It was Baptiste, and he was holding a long shiny blade to Max's throat. The boys and Musketeers stood quickly, hands upon their swords.

"Take your hands from your swords or the old man dies!" exclaimed Baptiste. His voice cracked with a tension that filled the room. "Now," he growled between clenched teeth. "Where *is* the book?"

Chapter Twenty-Three
Wee Musketeers to the Rescue

Grandpa Max appeared shaken. His narrow face was gray with fear. Baptiste dragged him through the kitchen. Eying D'Artagnan and the others with contempt, he pressed the knife harder against Max's skin. A slight trickle of blood trailed down Grandpa Max's neck.

"Let him go!" demanded Bobby.

"Produce the book!" growled Baptiste.

"There is no book—" pleaded Grandpa Max before Baptiste's sharp blade cut deeper into his skin.

"Stop it!" cried Bobby. "You're hurting him!"

"You, boy, are very smart." snapped Baptiste dismissively. "That is the idea." The guard's eyes narrowed viciously. "Now, bring me that book."

"There is no book," D'Artagnan said calmly. "You are quite mistaken—"

"Quiet, Gascon!" shouted Baptiste. "I heard you speak

of the book with my own ears!"

D'Artagnan started toward Baptiste. "If you release Max," he growled fiercely, "we will let you go. If you do not…" The Gascon tapped his sword. "…you will never leave this bakery alive."

"I will kill the old man!" Baptiste protested.

Athos looked down at the boys and winked before stepping between D'Artagnan and Baptiste. With one hand behind his back, Athos motioned for the boys to surround Baptiste.

"We have no book to give you, Monsieur Baptiste," said Athos calmly. "The game you play is a fool's game. Be smart or I will let the Gascon kill you."

Perspiration streamed from Baptiste's forehead and upper lip but it wasn't from the heat of the ovens. From the corner of his eye, he noticed the boys moving toward him.

"You send the children to stop me?"

"Maybe," said Athos, his voice remaining calm and even. "Maybe they are just getting out of the way so my large friend here can tear you apart." Porthos stepped forward. "Or, maybe my other friend will slice you in two." Aramis took his place by Porthos' side. All three Musketeers and D'Artagnan stood face to face with Baptiste.

Baptiste's knife fell away from Grandpa Max's throat. His hand glistened with sweat. The blade was still only inches from Max's skin. "Tell the boys to stand back!" he cried.

Athos and D'Artagnan motioned the boys away.

When Bobby stepped back he tripped and fell hard against a table. As he collected himself he looked absently at the ceiling. Just between he and Baptiste hung a small chandelier. Bobby quickly formulated a plan to end the stand off and save his grandfather. He motioned to Fritzy who was on the other side of Baptiste to shove Keith. Bewildered by his friend's odd actions, Fritzy shrugged and mouthed the word, 'what'?

Again, Bobby made a pushing motion and pointed toward Keith—this time Fritzy understood. Without hesitation he turned toward Keith and shoved him so hard he almost fell.

"Get out of the way!" Fritzy shouted.

"What's the matter with you?" snapped Keith.

Fritzy winked. "I said… you heard Athos, stay back!"

Keith smiled. "I don't have to—"

Fritzy shoved Keith again. In turn, Keith pushed him back.

"Take that, you big ape!"

Fritzy threw himself into Keith's midsection and both boys toppled onto the floor. As Baptiste turned toward the commotion, Bobby climbed up on the large wooden table and leaped into the air, grabbing onto the chandelier. Raising his feet, Bobby swung toward Baptiste. At the last second before impact, Baptiste turned to see the bottoms of Bobby's boots flying toward him. With a loud crunch, Bobby's feet struck the wide eyed Baptiste right on the nose. Baptiste dropped the knife as his head flew backward from the impact.

"Get him!" cried Bobby as he let go of the chandelier.

Before D'Artagnan and the Musketeers could move a muscle, Fritzy and Keith were firmly attached to Baptiste's legs causing him to lose his grip on Grandpa Max, who quickly dropped to the floor and rolled away to safety.

All three boys were on Baptiste; punching and pushing, fighting with all their strength. Overcome, Baptiste fell to his knees in defeat.

"Please make them stop!" cried Baptiste as he held his bleeding nose. "Oh my poor nose…not again!"

D'Artagnan and his companions pulled the fiery, young musketeers off the poor guard. The boys were still swinging wildly at Baptiste as they were less than gracefully dragged from the fight.

"Nicely done!" cried D'Artagnan, "You are a credit to your uniforms."

"Bravo!" exclaimed the Three Musketeers.

"Are-you-okay, Grandpa?" asked Bobby between rapid gasps for breath.

Max smiled and gave his grandson a hug. "Well done, boys," he said softly. "But I think that it's time we go home."

With Baptiste securely tied up in the cellar, Grandpa Max and the boys said their goodbyes to D'Artagnan, Athos, Porthos, Aramis and Xavier. The Musketeers couldn't say enough nice things about the boy's bravery and tenacity.

"We're going to miss you guys," said Bobby. "This was really cool."

Xavier looked troubled. "Are you boys cold again—?"

"No, no," replied Bobby. "It's not that… I meant—" Bobby felt something jab into his ribs. It was Fritzy's elbow. "Oh yeah…never mind," said Bobby while trying to keep from laughing.

Suddenly, the front door burst open and two figures

dashed into the kitchen.

"Jeanne!" cried Bobby.

"Planchet!" said D'Artagnan. "Where have you been?" The Gascon laughed heartily. It was plain to see that he was happy to see his lackey.

Planchet and Jeanne appeared to be exhausted from their search for Grandpa Max and the others.

"Once we realized that Monsieurs Athos, Porthos and Aramis were on the way to Paris," began Planchet, "we came here as quickly as possible."

"What of my father?" inquired Jeanne. "Can you get him released from the Bastille?"

Athos laughed loudly and then said, "I believe we have just the bargaining chip we need to obtain your father's release."

Jeanne tilted her head. Her eyes drooped sleepily. She looked as if she would drop to the floor at any second. "What do you mean?"

"What Athos means, dear," began Grandpa Max, who held a towel firmly against his wound, "is that we have one of Richelieu's officers tied up in the cellar…"

"…And there is no doubt," said D'Artagnan finishing Max's thought, "that His Eminence will be more than happy to make a trade and put this entire affair to rest."

"But what about the man from Meung?" asked Bobby. "Won't he want revenge?"

"Maybe," replied D'Artagnan. "But, I believe that Cardinal Richelieu will convince him to wait for a better time." D'Artagnan sighed. "So," he continued, "I will not worry until that *time* comes."

Bobby continued his inquiries. "And Lady de Winter?"

Athos glared at Bobby. "What do you know of this person?" he asked.

"I know that she was your wife," replied Bobby.

"How do you know this…?" Athos' voice trailed off. "Ah yes, the book."

Speaking of your wife," began Aramis, sounding more than a little puzzled. "I thought she was dead."

"As did I," replied Athos gloomily. "Nonetheless, we will deal with her later as well."

"But she works for Cardinal Richelieu, "said Bobby.

"We know," said Athos. "But let us not worry of such things."

D'Artagnan waved the subject away with a curt wave of his hand.

"Right now," he said brightly, "Our first task is to free Jeanne's father from the Bastille.

"Oh, this is wonderful," gushed Jeanne. Then looking back at Max's bloodied towel said, "But dear Grandpa Max, what has happened to your neck?"

"It's a long story," he replied.

"We will tell you all about it once Max and the boys are gone," said D'Artagnan.

"Gone?" gasped Jeanne. "Now?"

"I'm afraid so," replied Grandpa Max.

Jeanne turned to Bobby. "I will miss you very much, Bobby."

Bobby's face flushed. "I-I-I'll miss you too."

"Ooooooh la la," said Fritzy and Keith together.

"Aw, shut up!" responded Bobby.

"Are you two gonna kiss?" asked Keith.

"This I gotta see!" exclaimed Fritzy.

Bobby narrowed his eyes at his friends. Before he could say a word, Jeanne threw her arms around his neck and smashed her lips against his—Bobby's first kiss.

"Wow!" cried Fritzy and Keith together.

Grandpa Max grabbed the two boys and hustled them into the back room.

"Hey, wait a minute Grandpa Max," snapped Fritzy. "I want to see this."

Jeanne pulled her lips from Bobby's—they both blushed brightly.

"Maybe we will meet again some day," she whispered.

Bobby looked into her shining green eyes and whispered, "Maybe we will."

"Okay, Bobby," said Grandpa Max. "Into the back room. We're going home."

"Wait!" cried Xavier. "Do not go! We have almost forgotten. Monsieur Athos?"

Athos smacked his forehead with the palm of his hand. "Sacre Bleu," he shouted, "I almost forgot."

He rummaged through a small bag that had been lying on the table and pulled out three shiny blue uniforms with the crossed emblem of His Majesty's Musketeers.

"Now you are real Musketeers," said Athos.

"Forever," said Aramis.

"And always," grunted Porthos.

D'Artagnan saluted and smiled widely as Athos handed each of the boys his uniform.

"Thank you for everything," added the Gascon.

After a quick flurry of goodbyes, hugs and salutations, Grandpa Max and the boys were alone in the dim candlelight of the back room.

"Is everyone ready?" asked Bobby's grandfather. The three boys nodded their heads. "Place your hands on mine." They did. "Good, now repeat after me... All for one...One for all!"

"ALL FOR ONE...ONE FOR ALL!"

Chapter Twenty-Four
Now Where Did I Put Those Glasses?

The dimly lit room spun wildly around them. Bobby lost track of how many times the candle went spinning in and out of view. Faster and faster they went before the dark room appeared to melt away.

"Heeeeere we go again!" screeched Fritzy.

"Oh my stomach!" bellowed Keith.

"I'm so cold, Grandpa Max," shuddered Bobby.

"Don't be scared, boys," began a much calmer Grandpa Max. "It will pass in a moment."

Their world had spun out of control. Darkness enveloped the travelers and the cold became even colder.

"I can't take much more of this!" screamed Keith.

"Courage boys, courage," said Grandpa Max. "Just another second…"

It was less than a second before the spinning stopped

and they fell into a tangled heap. It was still dark, but the cold was gone. It was actually pretty warm and stuffy.

"Is everyone okay?" Grandpa asked cautiously. "Did we all make it?"

"Where are we?" asked Fritzy.

"I think we're back in Grandpa Max's closet," replied Bobby.

"I think I'm gonna hurl," squeaked Keith.

"Well," began Grandpa Max, "it seems as if we all made it safe and sound—except maybe for Keith."

Max reached up and found the string that led to the light on the ceiling and tugged it once. The tiny bulb filled the closet with a blinding light.

"Wow, that's bright!" exclaimed Fritzy.

"What am I sitting on?" said Keith.

"Lean to your left," said Bobby. Keith leaned over exposing a thick leather bound book. "It's *The Three Musketeers*," said Bobby as he snatched the book from beneath his friend.

Suddenly, the door flew open. It was Bobby's mom. All four sets of eyes stared up guiltily. Wearing her familiar housecoat, she glared at her father through horn-rimmed glasses.

"Where have you been?" she snapped. "I was just up here a half hour ago and you were nowhere in sight."

Grandpa Max struggled to his feet in the cramped quarters.

"You must have not looked in here, my dear," he said very calmly, "We've been here reading the whole time."

"You have?" she asked while looking down at the boys. Bobby and his friends smiled and nodded. "I could have sworn that I… Oh well. Anyway, Keith, your mother called; you were due home fifteen minutes ago!"

"Darn it!" growled Keith. "But, Grandpa Max, I thought you said—"

"Baptiste," said Max quickly cutting him off.

"Well I guess fifteen minutes isn't too bad—"

"Baptiste!" snapped Bobby's mom. "Who's Baptiste?"

"Just a character from *The Three Musketeers* dear," replied Grandpa Max.

"Oh, Dad," she said while shaking her head, "You and your books." Bobby's mom eyed the boy's new uniforms suspiciously. "Those aren't the ones that I made—"

"That's right, dear," Grandpa Max quickly interrupted. "I bought the boys new ones at the costume shop."

"Really? They look expensive."

"Not really," he replied giving the boys a sly wink. "Actually, they were almost giving them away."

The next day was like any other summer day, warm and long. The boys were still very excited over their adventure. Playing the Three Musketeers with renewed enthusiasm and real uniforms, they relived their adventure over and over again. Finally, as the day's shadows grew longer, Fritzy plopped onto the ground. He was frowning.

"What's the matter?" asked Bobby.

"Playing makes me miss the real Three Musketeers," he replied.

"Me too," agreed Keith. "And, we still don't have a D'Artagnan."

"Yeah, Bobby," continued Fritzy, "We're right back where we started."

Bobby sat next to Fritzy and Keith squatted just in front of his friends.

"But we got these great uniforms—"

"I know, I know but…" Fritzy's voiced trailed off. He was staring at something over Keith's shoulder. "Who's that?" he asked.

"Oh her?" replied Bobby who glanced in that direction. "She's the new kid who moved into the Bradley's old house.

Keith swung around. Now, all three boys were staring at the 'new kid.' The girl shifted her feet and played with her long, red pigtails trying to act as if she hadn't noticed the three sets of eyes glued to her.

"A girl!" growled Fritzy. "Why can't another guy move in…then we would have a D'Artagnan."

"Yeah," said Keith.

"Aw, she looks all right," protested Bobby as he jumped to his feet. "I'm gonna go meet her." He grabbed Fritzy and Keith by their arms and pulled them up. "C'mon!"

"Hi, I'm Bobby," he said. "And this is Fritzy and Keith."

"Hi," said Fritzy less than enthusiastically.

Keith just smiled and waved.

"I'm Judy," said the freckle-faced girl with a big toothy smile. "We just moved into town."

"Yeah, we know," said Bobby.

"Really?" she said surprised.

"Sure," replied Bobby. Then he shrugged and said, "Small town, y'know."

"Oh, I guess so..." Judy crinkled up her freckled nose. "Say, are you guys playing the Three Musketeers?"

Fritzy narrowed his eyes. "Yeah, how would you know—?"

"Oh, that's just one of my favorite books. I love D'Artagnan!"

Bobby looked at his friends and smiled.

Darkness closed in on Sky Harbor; the sun seemed to set much earlier this evening than the day before. Bobby sat comfortably on his grandfather's couch, paging listlessly through another one of the strange old books that Max had been given by the mysterious old lady. Grandpa Max was busy rummaging for something in the closet. He was making an awful racket.

"Now where could it be?" he muttered to himself. "I just saw it…"

"What are you looking for?" inquired Bobby absently.

Something fell, making a loud thud. "Ouch!" exclaimed Grandpa Max.

Bobby jumped up and peeked inside the closet. "You okay?"

Grandpa Max smiled sheepishly while rubbing his head. "Found it," he said holding up the old copy of *The Three Musketeers*.

"Why were you looking for that?" asked Bobby. "I'm not sure I ever want to see it again."

Grandpa Max's eyes twinkled like stars on a clear night. A mischievous smile split his craggy, narrow face. Bobby had seen that look before and it usually meant trouble.

"Aren't you in the least bit interested?" asked the old man.

"I guess…"

"C'mon Bobby," snickered Grandpa Max, his eyes still a twinkle. "Don't you wonder—just a little bit?"

Bobby's face flushed. "You know I do."

"So, what's the problem?"

Bobby narrowed his eyes and dropped heavily onto the couch.

"You *know* what the problem is, Grandpa." Bobby picked up the book he had been paging through and opened it pretending to read.

"Bobby!" Grandpa Max's smile widened.

"Okay, okay," snapped Bobby. "I'm afraid that we screwed it up."

"There's only one way to find out."

"Read it, I know…do we have to?"

Grandpa Max nodded.

"Okay, you win," said Bobby with a sigh.

Grandpa Max handed Bobby the book and rubbed his hands together briskly.

"Now," he said absently, "Where did I put my glasses?"

"You want to read it *now*?" asked Bobby.

Grandpa Max sat on the couch and retrieved the book.

"Okay," he said. "Not today."

Bobby smiled as he leaned back and opened up the

other book.

"So, what is that you're reading?" asked his grandfather playfully.

"*Robin Hood*," replied Bobby.

"I love *Robin Hood*."

"Me too." Bobby looked up at Grandpa Max; his eyes twinkled so brightly they seemed to glow. Bobby knew exactly what his grandfather was thinking.

"Oh no!" exclaimed Bobby. "Not again!"

"You know, I've been thinking about Robin and his merry men. We can leave right now. All we have to say is, welcome to Sher—"

"No! Give me '*The Three Musketeers*,' snapped Bobby. "I think I would like to read it again after all."

Grandpa Max winked at Bobby. "I thought you might change your mind. Now, where did I put those glasses?"

The End

Robert Bresloff's passion for history, adventure and the classics are brought together here in The Wee Musketeers. A former professional musician and songwriter, he is currently writing novels for young adult readers, fitness columns and magazine articles. Robert works as a Fitness Therapist and lives in a Chicago suburb with his wife Debra.